ST. MARK'S SCHOOL
7501 ADELPHI ROAD
HYATTSVILLE, MD 20783
301-422-7440

Cissy Funk

Cissy Funk

BY KIM TAYLOR

HARPERCOLLINS*PUBLISHERS*

Library of Congress Cataloging-in-Publication Data
Taylor, Kim.
    Cissy Funk / by Kim Taylor.
        p.   cm.
    Summary: Thirteen-year-old Cissy must discover what family
means to her as she struggles between her aunt and mother in
Depression era Colorado.
    ISBN 0-06-029041-2 — ISBN 0-06-029042-0 (lib. bdg.)
    [1. Family problems—Fiction.   2. Aunts—Fiction.
3. Mothers and daughters—Fiction.   4. Depressions—1929—
Fiction.   5. Colorado—Fiction.]   I. Title.
PZ7.T214815 Ci   2001   00-063204
[Fic]—dc21   CIP
                                                        AC

Typography by Andrea Simkowski
1 3 5 7 9 10 8 6 4 2
❖
First Edition

To
Jennifer Hirsh
&
Geneva Funk
(1904–1993)

I wish to give my heartfelt thanks to the following people, without whom this book would be no more than a dream: my editor, Antonia Markiet, for her incisive editorial comments and incredible creativity and support; my agent, George Nicholson, for believing in this book through thick and thin; Catherine Onder for her great enthusiasm; Dov Silverman for his mentoring during the first draft; and Jennifer Hirsh, who guided and shaped this novel from the very beginning.

Cissy Funk

PART ONE
RANSOM, COLORADO
1935

Chapter One

Cissy Funk dug under the house, grasping her knees to her chest. Ma's feet slammed and stomped back and forth in the kitchen. Cissy shivered. It sounded like Ma's heels would break right though the floorboards and crack her spine.

"Cissy! Get in this kitchen right now!"

She lay her head on the hard brown earth, trying not to let the dust make her sneeze. Reaching above her, she ran her finger over the sharp edges of wood where she had carved her name the week before. A sliver of hot white sun pierced through a cracked slat in the porch, and she shut her eyes against its heat.

"Narcissus Louise Funk! I swear to God, I will not be responsible for my actions!"

Two large, worn-out brown boots thumped hard in front of Cissy. Her older brother, Jonas, crouched down and peered at her with his yellow-green eyes.

"She's coming," he whispered.

"Shh. You ain't seen me. I ain't here."

"You gonna get whipped good this time if she finds you," Jonas said.

"Give you ten cents if you leave."

"She's gonna knock your head off and let it roll to Kansas."

"Leave now, or I'll tell about you sneaking out last night to meet Lucille."

"Cissy!" Ma yelled. "Get in here right now! I'm counting to ten. One . . . two . . ." She stepped out on the porch.

"Please, Jonas," Cissy begged.

"Four . . . five . . . six . . ."

Cissy dug her nails into her palms, feeling warm circles of pain.

"Jonas, what are you doing down there?" Ma asked.

Cissy imagined steam coming out of Ma's nose. Jonas's head popped out of her view as he shuffled onto the porch.

"Nothing. I lost my comb. Just looking for my comb."

"Are you a stupid boy who loses his comb outside?"

"Got a hole in my pocket."

"Have you seen your sister?"

"I believe she's collecting the eggs, Ma. That's where I seen her."

"Cissy!"

"Here, I'll go get her," Jonas said in a rush. "She's surely working awful hard. And you wouldn't want to upset all those hens now, would you?"

Jonas's big boots ran down the steps and around the corner. Then Ma's feet thudded back inside. Cissy held her breath.

When she heard only the pitch of the wind, she wriggled out of her hiding place. Jonas snatched her hand, pulling her across the dirt lot, checking over his shoulder along the way.

"Thanks, Jonas."

"Don't tell about last night, hear." He let go of her hand, spit in the dirt, then sauntered toward the creek.

Unhooking the chicken wire, Cissy pushed the hens out of the way, and set to dropping eggs into a basket, not even minding that three broke.

Maybe Ma would forget. Maybe it would be like last time when she started dancing to music in her head. She'd dropped her sewing, laughed, flung her arms wide, sung "Little Brown Jug," and spun Jonas around until he turned beet red with embarrassment.

The scuff of rotten wood startled her. The wire door swung open and Ma loomed, tilting to one side like a thin but sturdy silo beat by too much wind. The blue veins under her pale skin pumped with steady anger.

"There you are," Ma said. "I've been calling and calling. Didn't you hear me?"

"No, ma'am. I couldn't hear from here. Even when you yelled, I couldn't hear you."

"Now, why would you think I was yelling? You must've heard something."

"Not a thing. I was conjecturing."

"You were 'conjecturing,' Miss Big Word?"

"Yes, ma'am."

"Mmm-hmm." Ma placed a smile on her face, setting it on her mouth as if trying it on at a store. Sweet and soft, she said, "I walked into the kitchen for a nice glass of milk, and there was the milk jug laying on the floor. Split clean in half. Now, you wouldn't know what happened, would you?"

"No, ma'am."

"You're such a clumsy clog, I thought perhaps you'd accidentally knocked it over."

Cissy swallowed hard. "You dropped it last night, Ma. I heard you up. I heard it break."

"What are you talking about?"

"You remember, Ma."

"I don't like being accused of things I didn't do!"

Cissy's trembling legs caused the eggs to clack in the basket. Ma stepped forward, forcing Cissy back into the nesting shelves. The eggs tumbled from the basket and splattered in a circle around her feet. She looked down, but Ma pulled her head up, grasped both sides and squeezed like a vise. Cissy thought her brains would pop right out of her ears, but she didn't scream. She knew not to ever scream around Ma.

"Thirteen years old and can't do anything right!"

"I'm sorry."

Ma stalked back to the door. Her voice dipped low, hollow and weary. "Clean up those eggs, then come clean your mess in the kitchen."

Cissy hated that dead voice. It made her want to grab hold of Ma and shake her back into the living.

Chapter Two

Cissy and Jonas sat on the wide steps of the abandoned Coronado Hotel, watching dust clouds swirl out behind a passing truck on the way to somewhere else. Somewhere better.

"Look at this town, Cissy. Hot as Hades and no one thinks to plant a tree."

Cissy didn't even have to look. There wasn't much to see anyway, just a block of bleached wood buildings flung onto the plains like forgotten dice. The only true shade came from the disintegrating brick hulk of the Coronado. The worn-out sign above the Hasty Twins butcher shop squeaked and swung; it was so faded, the only writing left was *Twins*, added in red when Ruth Ann and Martha had taken over the shop from their father in 1915.

"I want to leave so bad, I can taste it," Jonas said.

Across the dusty street, Lucille's blond hair

bobbed in time to the radio playing in Mason's Emporium and Grocery. She stood behind the counter with her back to them, but every so often she'd turn her head and wink, then bob and sway a little more.

"Look at Lucille dance for you." Cissy pulled a light-brown strand of hair out of her mouth, then stood up and copied Lucille's movements, swinging her hips around, shaking her head. "Why, Jonas," Cissy said, imitating Lucille's high-pitched voice, "I just love you, Jonas. Can't wait to kissy-poo down by the creek."

"Ah, knock it off."

Cissy circled around him. "Baby, give me a love hug. Show me how much you care."

Jonas ran his fingers through his hair. "I told you to quit it." He stood up and threw her a nickel. "Go on over to the Blue Willow and get yourself a NEHI. I'll see you soon."

"How come you like her so much? She's a cow."

"Beat it."

Cissy smiled, and stuck the nickel in her pocket. She never spent money found or given, but slid it behind her photo of Douglas Fairbanks, Jr. She had at least three dollars saved behind that picture.

Across the street, Jonas now leaned against the counter, right up close to Lucille. He'd been sweet on her since grade school, and everyone knew he was going to marry her someday. Well, everyone except Ma. And Lucille's father, Mr. Grady Mason. Cissy wondered what Jonas was saying. Jonas caught her watching and mouthed an angry "Go away."

Kicking a rusty can down the sidewalk, she passed the Blue Willow Cafe. Inside, a few farmers sipped at coffee and picked at donuts. It was all anyone could afford anymore, and almost all the cafe sold. She walked by Jake's Bar, and heard the click of pool cues and smelled the rot of stale beer. Ransom sat in a dry county, but you'd never know it at Jake's. He'd served liquor all through Prohibition and beyond, and the sheriff was known to be his best customer. Cissy stopped under the Odeon Theater's marquee. Mack Dougherty stood high on a ladder, setting up the letters for the movie coming in the next day.

"Hey, Mack, what's playing?" Cissy shaded her eyes against the afternoon sun.

"*Broadway Gondolier*," Mack answered, his hands not missing a beat.

"What's it about?"

"You'll have to come see."

"Who's in it?"

"Dick Powell and Joan Blondell," Mack said.

"Is it good?"

"Is this twenty questions? I haven't seen it."

"If I clean up the aisles, can I come for free?"

"I'll think about it."

"Don't think too long," Cissy said. "The movie's only here a week. You know I do a good job."

"And you know I have to pay the rent."

"Mr. Roosevelt says we got to look out for each other."

"Does he, now?"

"Yes, sir."

"All right, Cissy. Two o'clock show tomorrow. But you can only stay for that show. If you want to see it again, you've got to pay."

"Thanks, Mack."

"How's your mama?"

"She's all right."

Mack wiped his hands on his pants and climbed down the ladder, smiling his lazy smile. He took a little hop on his good leg, and Cissy winced with him. Putting his weight on his left leg, the wooden leg that replaced the one he had lost to a thresher as a boy, caused him too much pain. Mack was a great guy. Not a picture went by he didn't let Cissy in for free. Once, he even let her watch three straight shows of *Cleopatra* when she didn't feel it was safe to go home. And he didn't ask any questions, either.

"You tell your mother she can see any picture she wants. On the house." Mack stepped back to take in the marquee. "Look all right to you?"

"Looks grand."

"Heard from your daddy?"

"Yes, sir. He's in Denver now."

"What's he sell again?" Mack asked. "Bibles?"

"Encyclopedias."

"That's right. The other good book."

"He's coming home soon," Cissy said.

"Oh?"

"It's true."

"Hmmm . . ."

"He's making money so's we can be rich. Sends some every month." Cissy squared her shoulders like she'd seen her father do anytime he told a lie.

"Your mother managing all right? Treating you good?"

Cissy swallowed. "Sure."

"You tell me if you need anything, Cissy. Anything at all."

Jonas came up from behind Cissy, a fool's grin plastered to his face. His eyes sparkled. "Hiya, Mack."

"Hey, yourself," Mack said. "Well, better get to work. Five o'clock show's coming up."

"See ya tomorrow," Cissy said.

"Don't be late. I'm counting on you."

"Yoo-hoo!" Dotty McPhearson flew down the street toward them, clipping shears in her hand.

She waved so fast, Cissy thought she might take off in flight.

"Your mama called on the party line. She said to get right on home."

Jonas shoved his hands in his pockets. "Why?"

Dotty's beak nose bobbed up and down. "Now,

I might have asked, if I was a gossipy type. But I keep myself to myself, so I'm just passing on the message." Dotty laid a hand on Cissy's arm. "You tell Rose hello from me. Tell her we missed her at the quilting circle."

Cissy nodded, and slid into step with Jonas. Far across the flat land sat the beginnings of a thundercloud, fearsomely tall and bright, overwhelming the blue and pink of the late afternoon sky.

"Look, Jonas. Ain't that a beautiful sight?"

"It's all right."

"There's something about those clouds. They're just so big, they make me feel like you and me and everyone else is just a speck of nothing. And it kinda makes bad things little specks of nothing, too. I can look at that cloud and think, well, there ain't nothing big as that can bother me."

"You're as crazy as Ma."

"No, I ain't. Don't ever say that."

He grunted. "That cloud ain't going to give us nothing but hot, dry lightning."

"Jonas, you think I could be a movie star? Not a big one like Claudette Colbert in *Cleopatra*, just a little dinky one?"

"If you're gonna be a star, you've got to wear something besides my old dungarees."

"I liked Lucille's dress today. Sky blue. Maybe she'll give it to me when she's sick of it."

"Cissy, you know we don't take any charity."

"I'm going to be a movie star, and that's that."

He laid an arm along her shoulders, allowing her to lean into him. "You're a crazy girl, Cissy."

A long, low roll of thunder shook the ground.

"That's out by the Tarnses' place," Jonas said. "Race you home."

He took off running, cutting across fallow land once filled with wheat. Cissy pumped her legs until she felt she was flying, her feet touching nothing but air. Still, Jonas stayed far ahead.

"Jonas!" she yelled. "Wait up! Don't leave me!"

But he was up the steps and through the door before she even made the turn by the vegetable garden.

Chapter Three

"Change your clothes. Sunday best." Ma's eyes glittered like a cat's, and her hair looked like spits of flame. "I had a vision. A daydream. We have to get ready."

"Ready? For what?" Jonas drawled.

Ma leaned in close to Jonas and whispered, "For something special." She ran her fingers lightly up and down his forearm. "Yes. Definitely something special."

Jonas pulled his arm away. "This was in your dream?"

"Dreams never lie." Ma slapped her hand on the kitchen table. "Cissy, go get dressed."

"But your dream, Ma," Cissy asked. "What was in your dream?"

"You dress like a lady. No dungarees."

"My dress is too small," Cissy said.

"And Jonas, you wear your suit."

"It's a hundred degrees out," Jonas said.

Ma narrowed her eyes. "Do what you're told. We don't have time for nonsense."

In her room, Cissy yanked hard at the dress's neckline, cutting off circulation to her forehead. She was sure half her hair had come out as she wiggled her way into the thin dress. She reached for her brush, and heard a rip under her armpit. Well, she sighed, at least it wouldn't pinch. She hated this frilly dress with its faded pink flowers and yellowed lace collar. But if Ma insisted she wear the one dress she had, then wear the dress she would. When Ma had a sign, you did what she said and didn't talk back.

Ma had a way of perceiving things, of finding omens not only in dreams, tea leaves, or a deck of cards, but in the way the moon shone on the rounded edge of the empty silo, or the way the wildcats sang. She had seen her best friend Emma Mason's death in the fold of a red-check table-cloth. Unfortunately, it was too late to save Emma from the tiny chicken bone that lodged sideways in her throat when she took up a song at the First Baptist Annual Picnic of 1933.

Ma hadn't always seen things. That had come after. After Violet's death. After the tiny coffin lay buried deep in the earth. Before Violet had come and gone, Ma had been like anyone else in Ransom. She quilted with her friends and smiled and did simple things like bake cakes and make homemade ice cream just because Cissy asked for it.

Now? Well, now was now. Now was a time to not ask for things.

Cissy closed her eyes. She didn't want to think about it. Thinking about it might unleash a fire of dark and sad and ugly things.

Cissy joined Ma and Jonas on the cracked and peeling green porch. Lined up in their Sunday best, they sat on the porch steps and waited. And waited.

Jonas tugged at his collar and tried to loosen his tie without Ma noticing. Cissy squirmed around, ready to burst from a need to visit the outhouse. Ma sat with her back as straight as the surrounding roads and kept her eyes glued to the front gate. The sun sank, the crickets took up a chorus, and still they sat.

Finally, under an ink-black sky, Ma stood up. "Well, I guess I was wrong. I'll make dinner." She shuffled into the house like an old woman, letting the screen door bang shut behind her.

"Damn dreams," Jonas whispered.

"It could've been real, though," Cissy said.

"Yeah, right." Jonas leaned back on the bench, stretching his long legs in front of him. "She ain't been to town in a year and a half. And suddenly she's calling on the party line? And what's it for? Spit."

"It could've been something good."

"And when has it ever been something good?

Don't people hate us enough already?"

"No one hates us, Jonas. Don't be exaggerating."

"People think we're strange. I've heard 'em talk about Ma and us. I'm lucky Hank would even give me a job at the service station. I bet no one else would've."

"No one else would've because there ain't any jobs. So don't be making up lies. I don't care what people say anyway." Cissy stood and stretched, her back stiff from sitting. She walked down the porch steps to the front gate, which swung and cracked against the posts of the wire fence. Clicking the gate shut, she looked up at the house. Spots of white paint glimmered against gray wood slatted like the boiled ribs of a skeleton. "It's kind of disappointing, ain't it?"

"What?" Jonas asked.

"I thought maybe something good might come. Or at least something different."

"She don't have visions, Cissy girl. She just sits like a spider and watches. Learns a lot from just watching."

A beam of headlights flashed across Jonas's face. He looked toward the beat-up Model T crunching its way up the gravel road.

The car sputtered to a stop. Mack hopped out, gave Cissy a wink, and said, "Got a surprise for you." He limped around to open the passenger door.

Cissy flew past Mack to open it herself.

"Aunt Vera! Jonas, look!"

Vera snapped shut her makeup case, dropped it into her purse, then stepped daintily to the ground. She grinned. "Why, honey, I hardly recognize you, you've grown so much. You've turned into a regular lady." She pulled Cissy into a tight hug.

"Can I take your bag up, Vera?" Mack asked.

"I got it," Jonas said.

Vera circled the car and grabbed Jonas by the arms. "Why, when did you get to be so handsome? Isn't he handsome, Mr. Dougherty? Of course he is."

Jonas's face flushed scarlet. He picked up Vera's heavy case and lugged it up the porch steps. "I'll get Ma."

"Would you stay for something to drink, Mr. Dougherty?" Vera asked. "I'd like to thank you for driving me out here."

Mack glanced at the house, then grazed his thumb along his jaw. "Another time."

Vera chucked her hip to one side. "I'll take that as a promise." She waved as Mack got back into the car.

"Come on, Aunt Vera." Cissy dragged her up the porch steps. "I can't wait to see Ma's face. She knew you were coming. She had this dream, see, and here you are!"

"Is that right?"

"Watch that top step, it's kind of loose."

Ma stood in the middle of the front room. "My

God," she whispered, "I was right." She smoothed her red hair, and pointed toward the kitchen. "I was making some dinner. I didn't think—"

"Hello, Rose," Vera said.

Ma crossed her arms. "Well, look what blew into town. I knew something was brewing, but I didn't figure it'd be you. So. Here you are." She gave Vera a stiff hug. "Cissy, go show Vera your room. You'll sleep on the couch." She untied her apron and took a swipe at the coffee table. "Excuse the mess."

"Come on, Aunt Vera," Cissy said, bounding up the stairs. "You'll love staying in my room."

She opened her door, clicked on the bedstand light, and waved Vera inside.

"Look at this room, Miss Cissy. Why, you've got all of Hollywood at your beck and call." Vera examined the lobby cards covering the walls.

"Mack gives me these photos once a picture comes through town." Cissy pointed. *Babes in Toyland*. Greta Garbo on a white silk couch in *Grand Hotel*. Jimmy Cagney's eyes peering from under a fedora. "See that one, Aunt Vera?" Cissy touched a color picture of Jean Harlow fanning herself on the porch of a rubber tree farm. "*Red Dust*. You see that one?"

"Did I see it? Five times. I can't get enough of that handsome Mr. Gable."

"This one's my favorite. There's Meg, and Jo, and Beth, and Amy, and Marmee. I sure loved

20

Marmee." Cissy swallowed. She didn't tell Vera that, when she slept, she dreamed it was Marmee whose arms held her. That sometimes, she could see Marmee as clear as she could see her own hand, and that she wished more than anything that Marmee would take her hand and walk her away from here. And then she'd have new sisters and a pretty room with a weeping willow to shade it in the afternoon. She lifted her chin. "And see here? I got a framed photo of Douglas Fairbanks, Jr. Signed and everything. I'll take it with me downstairs, if you don't mind. It don't ever leave my sight."

"My goodness. You're a special girl, Cissy. I'll tell you something truthful. There isn't anything more real than the pictures. Show you how to live properly and make you laugh your head off in these trying times."

"You got hard times, too?"

"No, honey, nothing like out here. We're in the money over there in the city. Everything's shiny bright and ready for the asking." She sat on the narrow bed and crossed her legs, letting one foot swing. "Reach in my handbag, Cissy. I've got a beautiful silk scarf made all the way in China. Let's lay it on the bedstand for some pretty color."

Cissy pulled wondrous things out of the bag. Genuine rhinestone earrings, a fan made out of peacock feathers, a small gold compact engraved with the initials *VF*, rouge, stockings. And an exquisite lilac scarf with a painting of a long-tailed wispy bird sitting on a branch, in front of a mountain range covered in gleaming snow.

Cissy held the silk to her cheek, then spread the scarf out on the bedstand. "It's beautiful."

"You like it?"

"I sure do."

"You can have it. Now, come sit right here"—Vera patted the bed—"and tell me what's gone on in your life. Got a fella?"

"No, ma'am."

"No one in particular you fancy?"

"No, ma'am."

"Don't call me ma'am, you make me feel old."

"Yes, ma'am, I mean, Aunt Vera."

"Vera'll be just fine."

"Actually, there is one boy."

"Tell, tell."

Cissy took a deep breath. "Rusty Tarns. On the farm across the creek from us?"

"I remember. With the big ears?"

Cissy smiled. "He don't know I like him. I just, well . . . What about you? You still hanging around with that fella you sent us a photo of?"

"Harry?" Vera sighed. "Oh, honey, that's a long, sad story. No need for it now. Why don't you help me unpack?"

Cissy watched Vera take clothes and clothes and

more clothes from her big case, all smelling of sweet perfume. Cissy didn't think everything would fit in her tiny wardrobe, but Vera somehow managed. She set her makeup and combs on Cissy's dresser, then lined her perfumes against the wall.

"How's Daddy?" Cissy asked.

"Frank? Same as he always is. I sure miss you, Cissy. Think about you every day. Why, sometimes, I'll be walking along the street and have to stop and say, 'I wonder how my little niece Cissy is today?' And now I see you're all grown up."

Cissy smiled.

"Of course, you still need to fill out a little. But you and I are going to take care of that. Count on Vera."

"Thanks."

"And I guarantee when we're through, Rusty's head will spin clear off his shoulders."

Cissy put up her hands to cool her blush.

Vera ran her fingertips over the tops of the perfume bottles, then picked one up and grabbed Cissy's wrist. "Here, try a little spritz of this."

Cissy jerked her arm away, then sniffed the perfume, hoping Vera hadn't noticed the bruise marks. "I'll bet Myrna Loy wears this."

"Mmm, gardenia," Vera answered. "Nothing like gardenia to soothe the soul."

"It's awful nice."

Vera cocked her head. "How is your mother getting on?"

"Just fine."

"It's a hard thing losing a child and then a . . . well, it's hard, that's all."

"Hey, you two, why don't you come down and join the party?" Jonas called up from the kitchen.

"A party? I'll go anywhere for a party. Come on, honey. We'll catch up later." Vera fluttered around the room, dabbed on a bit of dark lipstick, then took Cissy's hand. "We're coming, Mr. Jonas." She danced downstairs and plopped into the chair at the head of the kitchen table. "Isn't this nice! I am starving."

Ma set a plate of green bean salad, mashed turnips, and biscuits in front of Vera. She had taken down the bone china with the tiny blue windmills, plates last used the day of little Violet's funeral. Cissy slid her knife through butter already softened by the heat of the room, and smeared it on her biscuit.

"Beans. What a surprise." Jonas crossed his arms and leaned back in his chair.

Cissy wondered why Jonas bothered. Beans were a main staple in their household. The patch of garden out back fed them half the year, producing not only string beans and lima beans and wax beans, but corn, turnips, butternut squash, carrots, and canned tomatoes in the winter. Sometimes, though, she did imagine those stupid egg hens as a plate of steaming fried chicken.

Ma sat across from Vera and took a sip of lemonade.

"Aren't you eating, Rose?" Vera asked.

"Not hungry."

"Surprised to see me?"

"You could say that." Ma smiled. Like the Cheshire cat, Cissy thought.

"We been sitting out on the porch for hours," Cissy said. "Just waiting for something special. Ma had a dream, didn't you, Ma?"

"Did you, Rose?" Vera said. "Well, it's nice to see you. It's been a long time."

"Yes, it has. You look good, Vera."

"Why, thank you."

"How's Frank?" Ma asked.

Vera took a swallow of lemonade. "He's fine."

"He's coming home soon," Ma said. "He said so in the last letter."

"What letter?" Cissy asked. She'd have to sneak into Ma's room to retrieve it for her collection.

Ma rolled a fork between her fingers. "He's going to collect us all and bring us out to Denver."

Jonas set his biscuit back down on his plate. "When?"

"When he's good and ready, is when," Ma said.

"And when did you get this letter?" Jonas asked.

"Things are tight, you know how it is." Ma

rubbed at the worry lines on her forehead. "But Frank wants us to live in Denver. Isn't that right, Vera? He just needs to get settled and then he'll bring us all out."

Vera shifted in her seat. "Do you have any spirits around? I'd love a little drink."

"We don't keep any in the house," Ma said. "Get Vera some more lemonade, Cissy."

A deep silence fell suddenly, broken only by the wind rattling a window. Cissy figured Vera's presence had dredged up old and unhappy memories. She yearned to ask again about her daddy, but that would send Jonas into the blues and Ma into a rage of lies. With Ma's slippery truth, was there really even a letter?

Ma sighed, breaking the stillness. "We have families leaving every day now. Headed for Cal-i-for-nye-aye. I say good riddance, if they can't live through the tough."

"My best friend, Beth, and her family left just last March," Cissy said. "Farm went bust."

"Times are hard," Vera said.

"Times are times," Ma said. "We get three or four hobos stop here a week. Just stand at the backdoor and ask for work." Ma snorted. "Like there is any. I just tell them to move right along, we haven't anything extra." She leaned forward, her hand picking at a tiny rip in the tablecloth, like it was important to make the rip an actual hole. She stared at Vera for a full minute without blinking; her fingers ripped and disfigured the cloth.

Vera gave Ma a puzzled look. Cissy had seen the same look in other people's eyes when they talked at any length with Ma. Cissy remembered the last time Dotty McPhearson had stopped by, peach pie in hand, just trying to cheer Ma up. Mrs. McPhearson had shaken her head and practically run over Jonas and Cissy on her way out. She just couldn't take Ma's stare. Of course, Ma was much worse then. She'd been home from the sanitarium only a few weeks, had just lost Violet. She had developed a habit of staring into the middle distance with her mouth hanging open. Now, Ma watched everything, as if she could see through walls. Like she was always waiting, but wouldn't say for what.

She was an embarrassment.

Jonas stood up. "I'll clear the table."

"Why don't we sit in the front room?" Vera patted a curl in place, but it flopped right back down on her forehead. Vera walked down the hall, her arm around Cissy's waist. Jonas and Ma followed. "Jonas, come sit by my feet and I'll stroke your hair. That gorgeous red hair. You used to love me stroking your hair."

"That was a long time ago," he mumbled.

"Not so long ago." Vera moved to the easy chair. "Come over here, honey. Come sit by your aunt Vera." A tiny smile played the corner of her mouth.

"You're embarrassing the boy, Vera." Ma sat catty-corner on the end of the couch. "Leave him alone."

Cissy moved close to her aunt's chair, hoping to get a head rub herself.

Ma wrinkled her nose, sniffing the air. She got up from the couch, still sniffing, and followed the scent to Cissy. "What's that smell?"

"Aunt Vera let me try on her perfume. Gardenia. You like it?"

"Go wash, Cissy. You smell like a floozy."

"Oh, Rose," Vera said, "it's nice. Let her enjoy it."

"Cissy is thirteen years old. She does not need to flaunt herself."

"I'm not flaunting myself. I'm enjoying the perfume."

"She's certainly old enough to wear perfume," Vera said. "Why, I know girls hardly more than her age already married with a kid on each hip."

"I bet you do," Ma said.

Jonas leaned against the door frame and toed at the rag rug.

"Don't hover over there," Vera said. "You make me nervous. Come sit down. Let's plan our day for tomorrow." She glanced at Cissy. "I know. We'll go into town and buy Cissy a brand-new dress."

"Ma don't go into town," Jonas said. "Besides, we don't have money for new clothes."

Ma's eyes scraped the floor. "I have no need to go to town, that's all."

"What are you saying?" Vera's fingers, slowly combing their way through Cissy's fine hair, stopped midway on Cissy's scalp. "You never go into town?"

"She don't have to go anywhere," Cissy said. "Jonas and me do the errands."

"What about when you kids are in school?" Vera asked.

"There ain't been any school since last January," Jonas said, "because there ain't been any money for a teacher. I graduated last year, anyway. But there's a new teacher coming in the winter for Cissy."

"I been reading the encyclopedia, in the meantime," Cissy said. "I'm up to 'lemur.' Wish Daddy would send volume M to Z."

Vera bent forward in her chair, staring hard at Ma. "Rose? What's going on? Why don't you go to town?"

"You think I want those ignoramuses in town laughing at me?" Ma asked, sharp as a blade.

"That's the silliest thing I've ever heard. Who'd laugh at you?"

"People have long memories, Vera. Long and hard. Like elephants."

Vera wrinkled her brow. She rose from the easy chair and smoothed the wrinkles in her dress. "Pardon me while I visit the ladies' room."

"I'll take you, Aunt Vera. It's really dark."

"Thank you." She gave Cissy a squeeze and followed her down the back steps and along the path to the outhouse.

"If you reach your hand up you can use the blizzard rope," Cissy said. "It's awfully helpful when the dust storms come. There's a candle and matchsticks to the right of the door if you need them."

"I'll be fine." Vera swung the door closed. "Cissy?"

"Yes, ma'am?"

"It really is pitch black in here."

Cissy heard a match scrape and caught the yellow flame of the candle bleeding through the wood slats.

"There we are. Cissy? You still out there?"

"Yes, ma'am."

"Oh, no," Vera said. "I just got a splinter."

Late that night, Cissy lay on the couch watching a sliver of moon rise into a hole in the clouds. She had been told the moon was a poor man's version of the sun, but to her the sun didn't hold a candle to the moon. With night came peace. Moonlight brought her to a magical place where no one yelled and love was handed around like candy.

She picked up her photo of Douglas Fairbanks, Jr., with his graying mustache and suave eyes, kissed it, then shook it, listening with satisfaction to the clink of coins inside the frame. She set the photo on the table behind her, and reached under her pillow.

Placing a small tin box on her lap, she lifted the lid and picked out a pile of postcards. Postcards from Daddy. At the bottom of the tin she had pasted a photograph: Daddy leaning against a sleek Packard, his gold tooth silvery bright, his smile cockeyed. In the shadow of the car sat Ma, but she was only a dark image, and Cissy never paid her any mind. She ran her finger over the photo, feeling the warmth of the sun on Daddy's suit. She kissed her finger and touched it to his lips.

A creak in the house startled her. She shoved the letters back in the tin and pushed it under her pillow. She got out of bed and followed the rhythmic creaking down the hall to Ma's door. Through the crack, she watched her mother rocking the empty cradle that still sat in arm's reach of her bed. Ma's eyes were closed, and she hummed quietly. A whisper of a smile made her face slack and soft.

Cissy wished she could crawl in the cradle and have Ma sing lullabies to her instead of to the ghost of her baby sister, Violet. She felt a warm breath on her neck, and remembered the long sigh that had touched her face on the January morning when Violet's tiny coffin was lowered in the ground.

A hand touched her shoulder. Cissy relaxed under its softness. It was Marmee, of course.

Marmee always knew the best time to appear.

But when Cissy turned around, it was Aunt Vera, standing in her yellow chenille robe. She moved her hand to Cissy's cheek.

"Does she do this a lot?" Vera asked quietly.

"Yeah."

"I'm sorry, honey."

Cissy turned away. "I'm sorry, too."

Dear Beth,

Greetings from Dirt City, Colorado. How are things in sunny California? I sure miss you. My favorite aunt in the whole wide world is visiting. Even though she's my only aunt, she's still my favorite. She just under-stands me. Right away she asked about Rusty. I didn't tell her much, on account of propriety, and I certainly didn't tell her that I can see his window from my room and that I can't go to sleep until he turns off his light. She might not have understood that so much.

She even made Ma smile, and you know Ma ain't smiled since the funeral. But that's Aunt Vera—she can make you smile just because.

I sure wish you could be here, and we could all go to the pictures together. Aunt Vera loves movies just as much as you and me—and that's saying a lot!

Keep me in your thoughts. Someday we'll see each other again.

Yours always,
Narcissus

P.S.—That Flash Gordon pencil sharpener you gave me before you left sure has come in handy. . . .

P.P.S.—I read that Norma Shearer takes baths in milk. Ick!!!

Chapter Four

The next day, at the Odeon Theater, Cissy lifted the seats to their upright positions. She swept the floor. It was a small movie theater, but when the lights drifted low all that mattered was the magic on the screen.

She knocked on the projection room door and waited for Mack to give the all clear by waving his hand in the square window. When he did, she slid open the blue cotton curtain separating the front door from the rest of the theater.

Dotty fluttered in and handed her money to Cissy. She took a long strand of Cissy's hair in her hand. "You need a haircut, honey. And I don't mean a trim. Look at these stringies."

"It's all right."

Dotty stood on tiptoes to reach Cissy's face. "Maybe your aunt Vera can take care of things out there. Now that your mama, well, you know."

"No, I don't know."

"Come in the shop and I'll fix you right up," Dotty said with the pious look she usually reserved for Sundays. "Got that new Norma Shearer look that's all the rage." She closed her eyes tight like she had a bad case of gas, then opened them wide. She stared over Cissy's shoulder. "Why, Ruth Ann Hasty, I didn't think you'd make it."

Ruth Ann hobbled over and set a dime in Cissy's palm. She looked down her long nose and snorted. "How's Rose?"

Cissy clenched her teeth. How could she have forgotten Friday's matinee was Girls' Day on the Town, when Dotty turned away customers at the beauty parlor, and Ruth Ann and her sister, Martha, shut up the butcher shop early? Ma used to sit with them and laugh at ZaSu Pitts on the screen.

Cissy slammed into the projection room and slumped into the tall director's chair Mack sat in during the shows.

"You won't hear anything from in here." Mack moved a toothpick from the right to the left side of his mouth.

"Don't care."

"It's a musical."

"You ever wished you could kill someone?" Cissy asked.

Mack rolled up his sleeves and crossed his arms. "Anyone I know?"

"The witch brigade out there."

"Oh, *them*."

"Just because Ma don't go into town don't mean they can't come out to her. Ain't that what friends do?"

But Cissy knew why they didn't come, and she resented their freedom.

Walking home, Cissy stretched her arms wide, aiming her vision down one arm until it looked like she could touch the western horizon with her fingertip. She breathed in the good, dry air, thankful for a day without wind.

She hopped the back fence where it sagged close to the ground, then walked along the path to the vegetable garden. She pulled at a string bean, wiped it against her shirttail, and took a bite. It made a satisfying crunch, and she rolled the sweetness around with her tongue before she swallowed.

She scooped feed from the weathered box next to the house, opened the chicken coop, and spread the feed wide and fine so each chicken would get a fair share. Peck you to death for a scrap of food, those chickens.

The faraway sound of soft laughter caught her off guard. She raised her head, looking around the empty yard. No one by the outhouse; no one in the shadow of the old hay barn. Cissy walked around to the front porch and placed the laughter on the roof. Ma and Vera sat up there, faces golden in the first rush of sunset. Arms around each other, heads close, they looked like two schoolgirls telling secrets. Vera whispered something that made Ma cover her face with both hands, then lean against the house and guffaw.

"Come on up, honey," Vera said.

"You're late, Cissy," Ma called down. "Where've you been?"

"I had a sandwich with Mack, then helped with the second show."

"Well, come up here if you want to see something spectacular," Ma said.

Cissy ran into the house, skidded across Jonas's room, then climbed out the window. Ma pulled her down so she sat in the middle. The two women squeezed her in, their arms still slung over each other's shoulders.

Ma pointed at the sky. "Streaks of glory," she whispered. "Have you seen anything quite so fine of late?"

"No, ma'am. The clouds look set on fire, like they drifted too close to the sun."

"You remember, Vera," Ma said, "when you came to visit and you made me climb out on the roof with you? Lord, I was eight months pregnant with Jonas. Just to see a line of thunderclouds."

"Remember your hair? It stuck straight off of your head from all the electricity in the air."

"And yours was in those tight plaits."

"Mother nearly yanked my scalp off, the way she pulled my hair," Vera said. "Life is funny. We were so young and silly."

"Look, here comes Jonas." Ma cupped her mouth with her hands and shouted out, "Who's that fine-looking man walking down the road?"

Jonas grinned, and hopped the gate. He went to the pump in the front yard, pumped up some water, and rubbed his hands under it.

"Don't you drag grease in the house, Jonas," Ma called.

"What're you doing up on that roof? It'll cave in with all that weight."

"Very funny, Jonas," Vera said.

"We're watching the sunset," Ma said.

"Well, that sounds like more fun than a trip to Spain."

"Come on up, honey, and catch the last act," Vera called.

Jonas joined them on the roof and sat near Ma. They remained quiet as the gold darkened to purple and the first star began to blink in the night. Cissy sighed, feeling their combined breaths as they gazed at the sky. And Ma's smile made it the most perfect sunset Cissy could have ever imagined.

Chapter Five

"You need a dress and I need to shop. I've got a natural-born urge. But I don't remember it being quite so far."

Cissy and Vera continued down the gravel road toward town.

"Those fields used to be your grandpa Joe's," Vera said. "How your father convinced him to sell is beyond me."

"Daddy didn't want us growing up with dirt under our nails. Or that's what he said."

"Mmmm. Still . . ." Vera wiped her brow with a lace handkerchief that looked slightly worse for wear. "Honey, I've got to get off my feet a little. Isn't there any place we can catch a bit of shade?"

"We can go across the field and sit under the trees by Gold Creek."

"Across that field?"

"Uh-huh."

"Well, it'll feel nice to dip our toes in the water. When Frank and I were little we used to come down to that creek. Your daddy would catch crawdads and tadpoles and anything that moved. How about you kids?"

"There ain't no water. Hasn't been any water there for three years, except when it flooded last April for a week. But if you can make it to town, we can get a cream soda at the Blue Willow."

Vera's drooping shoulders perked up at the vision of a cool drink. She dabbed at the beads of sweat sitting on her upper lip.

"Why don't you take off those heels?" Cissy asked.

"A lady never removes her shoes in public. It creates the wrong impression."

"That's the stupidest thing I ever heard."

"Honey, it's a law to abide by." Vera limped her way through the stubby grass.

Cissy shrugged. "If you want to dodge prairie dog holes with every other step, then I won't say one more word about it."

"On second thought, I think I *would* like to sit, honey. Those trees look so inviting."

"All right."

They moved across the field toward the cottonwoods and sat on the ground where it sloped to the dry creek bed. The mottled brown leaves of the trees clicked together in the breeze.

"Ten miles from here"—Cissy rolled up her sleeves, then pointed west over the creek—"there ain't nothing wrong. They've got sugar beets and corn and cattle all over the place."

"I saw it on the way in. It's funny, how the crops just stop. Just a field of corn bumped up to a field of dust."

"Strange, ain't it?"

"Cissy, I've been curious. Doesn't anyone come out to visit? Rose used to have such good friends."

"No, ma'am."

Vera sighed. "Shame."

"Why?"

Vera touched Cissy's rolled-up sleeve. "What happened to your arms, honey?"

Cissy glanced away, sifting dirt through her fingers. She wanted to tell. Vera made it so easy to tell. But if she did, she might get caught. And there were times, she had to admit, that she'd been at fault herself. It was all too complicated. If she told on Ma, she also told on herself. So she said nothing.

"Did your mother do that to you? Or Jonas?"

"I'm a little clumsy, is all. Ran myself smack into the henhouse. It was a funny sight; you oughtta have seen it."

"Must've been a laugh."

Cissy stood up, brushing the dirt from her pants. "You ready to go?"

Vera rose, nodded, then pulled Cissy close. "Sure, honey."

"Lucille don't like me," Cissy whispered to Vera. "She thinks I'm going to steal something. It's on account of those crime magazines she reads all the time. But a person could walk off with the entire men's coat section, a block of ice, and a bag of feed before she'd notice something was amiss. If Jonas was here, though, she'd be flipping her tail like a mule with flies."

Vera stood on tiptoe to see over the top of the dress rack. Sure enough, Lucille had a magazine flung open across the counter, and her cheeks burned pink with the excitement of her reading.

Cissy pulled a burgundy cloche low over her eyes, then stuck her tongue out at Aunt Vera. "How do you like it?"

"Not your color."

"What about for Ma?"

"Burgundy on a redhead? Definitely a faux pas."

"A foe paw? What's that?"

"A big no-no. In French."

"I'm stealing this hat, Lucille," Cissy yelled out. "Hope you don't mind, you foe paw."

Lucille licked her forefinger, sighed, and

turned a page of her magazine.

Cissy set the hat back on the shelf, and followed her aunt past the almost empty racks of women's clothes. Vera ran her hands over the stacks of men's shirts, every so often looking at the size label at the neck.

"We should get Jonas a shirt, Cissy. Can't have him look so raggedy, now, can we?"

"You can get it for him, but that don't mean he'll wear it."

"He'll wear it. This one looks about right. Plain white. You can't go wrong with white."

Cissy wanted to get something for Ma, some little thing that would please her. She remembered the way Ma had laughed, up on the roof, and she thought that maybe Ma was back to being just Ma. She looked around the large square room, past shelves of ties and purses, past Vera now holding a dress up to her body and admiring it in the mirror, past the hats and scarves and high heels. Then her eyes set on the perfect present, a thing luxurious in and of itself, a gift that was special because it wasn't coming at Christmas. She checked the coins in her pocket. Yes. Just enough, but no more. She walked over and picked up a pair of sheer stockings.

"What do you need those for, Cissy Funk?" Lucille asked.

"My gosh, you're actually talking to me?"

"Tell your brother I can't meet him later, all right?"

"Why not?"

Lucille raised her head, and Cissy swore she'd be pretty if her eyes didn't have a touch of the demon to them.

Lucille winked and cut a sly little smile. "Just because."

"He'll want an explanation."

"I'm sure he will, but that doesn't mean he'll get one. You have money for those stockings?"

"No, I thought I'd steal them while you were looking at me. You didn't know this, Lucille, but Ma Barker's my real mother, and I'm apprenticing in the trade."

"Even Ma Barker dead is better than your crazy mother. That'll be fifty-two cents."

Cissy felt her face flush red. "You don't know anything about anything."

She looked over at Vera picking through the costume jewelry, not paying them any mind. Cissy slapped her money on the counter. Her collection of buffalo nickels clicked and banged and rolled across the counter glass.

"Put your money away," Vera said. "I'll get that."

"That's all right. I have money for it."

"We need to get you a dress, honey. You look

like a hobo in those pants."

"Maybe next year. I'm fine for now. I'm having a hard time breathing in here, though, what with Lucille's awful smell."

"But, honey—"

Lucille glared at Cissy and said real loud, "The Funks don't have enough credit for a dress."

"I'm ready to go when you are, Aunt Vera. I'll be outside."

"Don't forget to give your brother my message," Lucille said.

Cissy sneered, turned on her heel, and stomped out the door. She paced back and forth as she waited. Vera finally joined her, a package clutched to her chest.

"How in the world can she like my brother and treat me like a bug on shit?" Cissy said. "It ain't right. And she didn't even wrap these stockings for me."

"She's just jealous, honey."

"Come on, Aunt Vera, let's go to the picture show."

"Hold your horses for a minute. I got you a present."

Cissy stopped in her tracks. "You did?"

Vera nodded.

"Can I see it?" Cissy asked.

"Well, it'd be better to show you at home. It's a private thing."

"You mean, just between me and you?"

"Yes, indeed."

"What is it?" Cissy imagined a pair of sparkling earrings she could flaunt around to show everyone she wasn't the trash they thought. Or maybe it was fine lace gloves, just right for a midsummer day.

Aunt Vera crooked her finger and motioned. Cissy leaned in close, hearing the rustle of her aunt's deep-red dress as a quick gust of wind shifted by.

"It's a brassiere, honey," Vera whispered into Cissy's ear. "You need to start wearing a brassiere."

Cissy slumped her shoulders in an effort to hide her growing chest, wanting to disintegrate into smoke and drift away. But she nodded, and gave Vera a small kiss on the cheek. "Thank you, Aunt Vera."

"Stop calling me that. It's Vera. Just plain Vera. I'm only twenty-eight, for goodness' sake." Vera tucked Cissy's arm under hers. "Let's go see the picture show."

In the theater, Cissy thought only of her hand grasped softly and tightly by Aunt Vera's. She wished they could stay that way forever.

Chapter Six

As they left the movie house, a strong wind slammed the door shut behind them. Vera pulled a scarf from her bag and wrapped it around her head. They saw the blackness at the same time, the steaming, roiling black of a dust storm sitting like the Devil on the buildings across the street.

"Oh, my God," Vera said.

"We've got to go," Cissy said. "We got to get to Ma before—" A funnel of piercing sound threw her into high gear. "Now!" She jumped the steps, dragging Vera behind her. The sky gleamed clean in the west, dirty black in the east. For a split second Cissy felt she was running in two worlds. If she could just make one giant leap, she'd be out of this danger.

She put her head down and pushed into the gusts, letting go of Vera's hand to cover her eyes. She lunged across an open field, but the dark came fast, swirling around her. She didn't know which way she faced, and she'd lost Vera.

"Vera! Aunt Vera!" she screamed, over and over, but no sound could penetrate the awesome gloating moan of the wind.

The gust pushed Cissy to her knees. She tried to crawl, tried to dig her nails into the shifting dirt. Powerless, she balled up, shielding her eyes with one hand to keep out the grit, the other hand gripping the stockings to her belly. Damn Lucille for not wrapping them.

"It'll pass," she whispered. "It'll pass."

Her hair whipped around, caught in her mouth, slapped her eyelids. The dirt pierced and stuck to her skin. Something hit her back, then junked away.

Suddenly, two strong hands lifted Cissy to her feet and pushed her forward. The lurch told her it was Mack, and she clung to him.

The moan of the storm competed with the cracks and thumps of doors slamming shut over and over. A windowpane shattered. And then another. Cissy, her shoes filled with dirt, grabbed harder at Mack. She sensed other people leaning against the thick wind, trying to find shelter. Dark figures against a darker sky.

Mack pushed Cissy through the side door of the theater, and the sudden, still air made her feel queasy. She slid down the wall, rasping, wiping at the grime that stuck like sandpaper to her cheeks.

Mack leaned against a chair. "Don't give me a fright like that."

"Thanks, Mack."

"You should have stayed put."

"I thought we could make it."

He shook brown grit from his hair. "Ah, heck."

Cissy's heart slowed. Her stomach steadied. She still clung to the stockings: dirty, crushed, but luckily, not torn.

Then her brain snapped to. "Where's Aunt Vera? We got to find Aunt Vera."

"She's in the washroom. She had enough sense to turn around."

"Now, that was really something!" Vera pranced down the aisle toward them. "If it wasn't for Mr. Dougherty here on the lookout for strays and stupid women, we'd be buried under a pile of earth somewhere," she said.

"It was nothing," Mack murmured.

"You saved Cissy's life, Mack. You should have seen him, Cissy. Not a second after he let me in the door, he raced out to get you. Don't call that nothing."

"Look, Mack, can you give us a lift to the house?" Cissy asked. "Ma's scared of these storms, and I've got to see if she's all right."

Mack nodded.

"Tell me if I'm being forward now, would you?" Vera asked. "I'd like to have you come out to my sister-in-law's. Join our little family for supper some evening. As a way of saying thanks."

"You're being forward," Cissy said.

"No, she isn't," Mack said.

"You'll have to ask Ma first. She might not—"

"It'll be fine with Rose, I'm sure," Vera said, "We'll ask her when we get home."

"I'd be happy to give you both a lift out. As soon as the dust settles."

"Why, thank you, Mr. Dougherty," Vera said. "We'd be most obliged."

Chapter Seven

"Go get your mother, honey," Vera said.

Cissy scrambled out of Mack's Model T. A curtain drew back from the front window of the house, then quickly dropped. She climbed up the steps. The door swung open before she reached it, and Ma flew out at her, eyes narrow with fury. She stretched her arm toward Cissy, grabbing a wrist and pulling her inside. An inch of dirt lay on everything, and Cissy couldn't even see the rug under her feet.

"Ma! Ma, Mack's outside, Mack's—" Cissy felt the sting of a slap across her right cheek. She tugged hard to get away from the squeeze on her wrist that seemed to scrape her bones against each other.

"What the hell is wrong with you?" Ma said. She slapped Cissy again. "How could you leave me here during that? I hate the wind, I hate—"

"Stop! Mack's outside, Ma!"

"Sit down!" Ma shoved her onto the sofa, then headed toward the door.

Ma stumbled to the door and slammed it shut. Cissy wiped at the tears on her cheeks. She heard Mack's Model T sputter away.

Vera opened the door and walked into the front room. "Wild times, Rose, wild—"

"You see this stupid girl?" Ma marched over to Cissy, grabbed her upper arm, and dragged her to her feet.

"Rose—"

"She left the chicken coop unlatched." Ma's breath was sour with anger and fear. "Unlatched! The chickens are God knows where."

"I'm sorry, Ma. I didn't—" Cissy, ducking a blow, dropped to her knees.

"Rose, don't." Vera pulled at Ma's free arm.

"You stupid girl," Ma said, "how do you think we'll survive without those eggs?"

Cissy expected the kick before it came, but it still knocked the breath out of her.

Vera wrapped her arms around Ma's taut body, using all her weight to get her off Cissy.

"Stay out of this, Vera," Ma said. "It's nothing to do with you."

From far away, Cissy heard the screen door creak open, then saw Jonas crossing toward the women.

"Jonas," Vera said, her voice strained. "Jonas, help me."

"I got some of the hens, Ma," he said. "I found 'em under the house. We probably lost a couple in the storm."

Ma drew deep breaths. Vera loosened her grip, but placed her body between Ma and Cissy.

"Good, Jonas," Ma said. "That's my boy."

Cissy braced herself up on one arm, feeling a sharp spasm low on her ribs.

"Cissy, honey—" Vera kneeled next to her.

"Stay away from her," Ma warned.

Vera backed away at the threat in Ma's voice.

"Come here, Cissy," Ma commanded.

Cissy hesitated, held her ribs, slowly stood up, and nearly doubled over with pain. Vera stepped toward her.

"I said to stay away." Ma swallowed.

"I didn't get the eggs this morning," Cissy mumbled.

"What's that?"

"I remember latching the door. Yesterday. It was the wind!"

Ma took one step forward. "You're a liar! Get outside and find the rest of those chickens!" She jerked toward Cissy, pushing Vera aside when she tried to get in between. Ma's hand snaked out, grabbing Cissy's hair, pulling her toward the kitchen door.

"Rose! Let her go!" Vera yelled.

"I know the dust storm scared you, Ma, but it's

all right now." Cissy felt as if the skin on top of her head would come clean off in Ma's hands. She twisted and pulled, but that just made the pain worse. If only she could be strong enough to fight back, if only she could think of something to say that would stop this.

"Stop it, Ma!" Jonas said.

Ma dragged Cissy through the door, slamming her head against the hard edge of the door frame.

"That hurts, Ma!"

"You think that hurts? I'll give you something to cry for." Ma's hand swung back and Cissy relaxed her body, surrendering again, knowing a loose body would make it hurt less. She saw the fist come down, felt the connection that made blood spurt from her mouth, felt herself turn, smash a shoulder into the cupboard. A cup fell in front of her and shattered.

Vera pressed her hand against Ma's chest, pushing her away from Cissy. "Rose, stop it!"

Ma stared off into nothingness. "I hate the wind." Suddenly, she snapped her head, icing Vera with her stare. "What are you looking at?"

"Nothing," Vera answered, backing up one step.

"What are you *looking* at?" Ma spit out.

Jonas gently helped Cissy to her feet. "Come on." He wrapped an arm around his sister and led her to the door.

"You find those chickens, Cissy." Ma pointed a

long finger. "Every single one of them!"

"Why do you have to do this, Ma?" Jonas said. He looked over at Vera, his face filled with humiliation.

"You left me alone. Everyone leaves me alone," Ma said.

Vera's cool arm slid along Cissy's shoulder.

"That's it," Ma yelled. "Spoil the child. Make her a little baby!"

Vera tensed her jaw. "If you touch her once more while I'm here, Rose, I'll see to it they put you away again."

Ma snorted.

"Would you like that?" Vera asked.

"You can't do anything to me. I know you, Vera."

"Well you just try me."

After gathering up the chickens, Jonas, Vera, and Cissy returned to the house and cleaned. Dirt floated through the air, resting on plates and pots. It hid between floorboards, was tucked in the pockets of clothes, stuck to the edges of stinging eyes. All the dirt had pushed its way through a half-inch crack in the kitchen window.

Vera sniffled, sneezed mightily a few times, and continued to wipe every cupboard in the kitchen. Jonas swept the floor. Cissy took a rag to the table-tops. She bent slowly in an effort to soften the pain of her bruised rib. They tiptoed past Ma's locked bedroom door. Best to let her be.

Cissy dusted the coffee table, plainly remembering latching the gate. Wiping down the lamp, she saw herself just as plainly leaving the gate swinging open and being too lazy to go back and shut it. By the time she passed Vera in the upstairs hall, she was sure she had left it open.

She grasped the stair rail, moving so as not to jar her body. She hurt everywhere, but mostly in her heart. She held her breath until she had passed Ma's door. Cissy heard Ma crying. Good, she thought. She should feel bad.

Suddenly, the door creaked open, and Ma's red eyes peered through the crack. "Cissy? Come sit with me." Ma lowered herself to the bed, her eyes red and swollen. "I'm so sorry. I don't mean to do the things I do. Really, I don't." She hid her face in her hands, and her shoulders rocked with grief.

"I promise I'll check the gate," Cissy said. "Every day."

"I hate dust storms. You know I hate them. They make me feel all alone."

"Don't cry, Ma." There her mother sat, small and scared, and Cissy saw, for an instant, the old Ma. The one who kissed Cissy to sleep when she was a little girl. She thought if she could just do something to keep her there, this old Ma, things might be all right again. She remembered the stockings. Yes. A present. Cissy reached into her pocket, past the bloodied rag she'd held to her lip, and pulled out the rumpled stockings. "Here, please don't cry. Look, I got you a present in town." She unraveled the wadded, sheer fabric, and lay it in her mother's lap.

Gently tracing the back seam with her finger, Ma held the stockings up so the silted light filtered through. Then she dropped her hands back in her lap.

"Don't you like them?" Cissy asked.

"I have tried. God, I've tried," Ma whispered. "You love me?" She turned her head toward Cissy, and fixed her with a stare. Her eyes were hard as glass and just as cold. The old Ma was gone again.

Cissy felt a bead of fear and sweat roll slowly between her shoulder blades. "Yes, ma'am."

"Say it. Say you love me."

Cissy swallowed. "You know I do." She pulled at a piece of hair, twisting it around her fingers. How far to the door? How far to Vera?

"You'll never leave me, will you? Never leave me alone in a dust storm?"

"No, ma'am, I'll never leave you."

Ma's eyes released Cissy, and her mouth turned up in a little grin.

Vera pushed open the door. "I warmed up some vegetable soup. Here, Cissy, you go on out. I need to talk to your mother a minute."

Cissy walked into the hall, and Vera shut the door tight.

She tried to listen to what they were saying, but the women's voices softened to harsh murmurs. She walked to the kitchen, which sweltered and steamed in the heat of the day. The bubbling soup didn't help.

Jonas stirred the soup in the big iron pot on the stove. "I hate her, Cissy. I should have stopped her. I should have done something for you."

"Yeah, well, it was my fault. And you got the chickens." Cissy sat down at the table.

"Why do you always take the blame? It wasn't your fault, not this time and not all the other times." Jonas slammed the spoon on the counter, then sat in the seat next to her. "I can't take it no more. I really can't. I think if she does one more crazy thing, I'm going to kill her. And I mean really. I feel I might just wrap my hands around her neck and squeeze until there's nothing left." His hands shook. "I heard of this new deal, the Civilian Conservation Corps. Lots of boys are joining. Earning money."

"You can't go." He couldn't. Because if Jonas left, he would be taking a piece of Cissy's heart. She wondered if it would actually beat without him. And she'd be alone with Ma.

"I got to someday. And I been worried about you. That's why I ain't gone. But Vera's here now, and she ain't afraid of Ma like you and me."

"Vera ain't staying forever," Cissy said.

"I think she is. She got laid off from Gates

Rubber Company. She ain't got money and she ain't got no place else."

"How come she didn't tell me that?"

Jonas got up and stirred the soup. "Because it's all secrets and lies around here, that's why. Just secrets and lies. Welcome to the Funk family."

Dear Beth,

Sorry I haven't written lately. I've been a bit under the weather. Haven't even felt like watching for Rusty's light at night.

I think my aunt Vera has a dreadful secret she ain't telling. She brought enough dresses to last till doomsday, and Jonas said she lost her job. I'll bet it's to do with some tragic love, and I'm sure going to try to find out the details.

Did you read of that little boy in Oklahoma that suffocated during a dust storm? I keep waiting for someone to kick the bucket here (I even had a close call myself, but don't you worry, I'm fine). We lost a couple of laying hens in that last storm, suffocated just like that little boy down in Oklahoma. Dirt, dirt, and more dirt!

Write soon.

Yours always,
Narcissus

Chapter Eight

Secrets and lies. The words stuck in Cissy's head like glue. She wanted to know what they were; she *had* to know. Cissy rapped on Jonas's door.

"What do you want?"

"Let me in," she whispered.

"I'm busy."

"I need your help."

"What for?" He pulled the door wide enough for her to slip through.

"Never mind what for. Just stand at the top of the stairs and start whistling if Ma or Vera come inside."

He sat down on his narrow bed, his long legs slung wide. "Don't cause any more trouble."

"Look, I'm going to give you some money so you can treat Lucille to a picture show."

"What are you up to?"

"Don't look a gift horse in the mouth, Jonas.

Just stand at the top of the stairs and watch out. I got to find something. Come on, Jonas, make up your thick mind."

"Give me the money first."

"You think I'm stupid? Just go be a lookout."

"Sometimes I worry about you, Cissy."

"Well, go worry by the stairs."

Jonas stood up, and Cissy had a fleeting fear that this was the last of their time together. She saw a brief, clear picture of him walking away across the plains until he was no more than a black dot on the horizon.

She slid along the short wall between his room and Aunt Vera's, pushed open the door, and snuck inside. She felt like a thief, and her heart beat in a loud, steady thump. She didn't know what she was looking for. She wiped her palms on her dungarees.

She wanted to find Vera's secret. She clicked open the wardrobe and ran her hand along its base; her hand came in contact with nothing but shoes. Maybe Vera kept her secrets hidden in a box or a tin. She turned to the dresser, but the drawers contained only soft underthings.

She made a quick turn around the room. Something had to reveal Vera's story. She slid a hand under the pillow, flipped through *The Good Earth* on the nightstand. Her foot slid under the bed and hit something hard. Vera's suitcase.

Cissy knelt down and pulled the smooth brown

leather case toward her. She heard Vera laugh; her heart bounced into her throat. She froze with the lid halfway open, but no signal came from Jonas.

A photo album lay in the bottom of the case. She set it on her crossed legs, and flipped through yellowed photos of old people and babies draped in lace.

Then her hands slowed. A girl's dark eyes stared out at her, burning a hole into Cissy's heart. Probably eleven or twelve, and already bold. It could have been a picture of herself. "RH Stempel Studios, Denver" was stamped in the corner. The dark eyes and hair, the layers of ivory lace: It must have been Aunt Vera as a girl.

In another photo, a group she knew well sat beneath the big cottonwood tree down by the bend in the creek between the Tarnses and the Funks: Daddy's mouth was open wide, caught in a laugh, his arm draped over Jonas's rail-thin shoulders. Ma leaned into Jonas, her eyes filled with laughter. And there she was, curled against her mother's feet, her head thrown back in joy. A bitterness burned the back of her throat. It was a time before Violet. Violet. The cause of all the mess.

She turned the page to a picture of herself as a tiny baby as ugly as old Al Capone. Her hands turned pages with more photos of herself: crying on the porch steps on her first day of school, her first haircut, sitting on Vera's lap when she came for Cissy's fifth birthday.

A tear dropped from Cissy's cheek and landed on the picture. She wiped it away, her thumb bearing down on her face, trying to wipe it clean out of the picture. She was no longer that girl. She wanted to rub herself out of every picture that showed how life had once been. The past tugged at her all the time, draining her of any strength she had left. She didn't want to remember what it used to be like. Yet she wanted it completely. She felt the confusion of being tossed between two very opposite ideas. She dreamed of Daddy coming home, and yet that same longing made what was right around her too much to bear. And she had to bear it.

Turning past more photos, Cissy saw Vera's hair change from braids to a bob, to the rowdy curls Cissy knew. There was a recent picture of Daddy and Vera and a woman with hair as white as Jean Harlow's. Cissy touched Daddy's face. He was broader than in the picture she had of him, and his hair seemed thinner. She wondered when he started to look so old. She hesitated, then pulled the photo out of its four-corner mooring and stuffed it down her dress.

Cissy turned the thick paper and stopped at a picture of the woman with white-blond hair standing next to a marquee and pointing up at the name: Maxine LaTrelle.

Cissy flipped back to earlier pictures, and recognized the same woman. Cissy shivered. Who was she? Maybe she had something to do with Vera's secret. Maybe she'd been Vera's best friend and maybe Harry fell in love with the blonde, and out of love with Vera. And Vera had such a broken heart she had to flee Denver. Cissy smiled. Yes, that was it. It would sure make a good motion picture. She pictured the marquee: Myrna Loy, Miriam Hopkins, and Tyrone Power.

Jonas's whistle cut into her. She dropped the album into the suitcase, shoved it back under the bed, and got to her feet.

Vera swung open the door. She frowned and scanned the room. "What are you doing in here?"

"Um, I wanted to get a lobby card to tack up downstairs by the couch. I couldn't decide, though, between Laurel and Hardy or Claudette Colbert."

"I know it's really your room, honey, but a woman's bedroom is sacred space. One should get permission before entering."

"Is that a rule to live by?" Cissy tried to laugh past the block in her throat.

"It's a request."

"Yes, ma'am." Cissy lowered her head and stepped around Aunt Vera.

"Cissy?"

"Yes, ma'am?" She couldn't pull her eyes from her feet.

"You forgot to take a lobby card."

"I'll . . . I'll get it some other time."

Vera shut the door with a soft thud, leaving Cissy staring like an idiot at the worn hallway floor. Her brain whirred with images; the girl with the burning eyes and the woman with the white-blond hair swam through them all.

Chapter Nine

Standing on a chair in the middle of Vera's room, Cissy ran her tongue over the sharp points of the pins stuck between her lips. She wanted to sigh a big, bored sigh, but feared swallowing the pins. She shifted her bare feet, and the chair she stood on rocked to the left. She reached out a hand to balance herself on Vera's shoulder.

"Pin," Vera said.

Cissy took one from her mouth and set it in Vera's palm. From her vantage point near the window, she saw Jonas fiddling around with the hinges on the outhouse door. She followed Vera's hands as they pinned the hem of the dress, marveling at the efficiency of her fingers.

Vera stretched out her long, strong fingers for another pin. Cissy placed her palm against her aunt's, comparing their breadth and shape and length. Though her hand was slightly smaller, the likeness was obvious in the curved pinkies. It seemed to Cissy she was touching her own, older hand.

Vera pulled her hand from Cissy's. "Are you going to admire your hand all day? Or are you going to give me a pin so I can get this dress sewn in time for the social?"

Cissy gave her the last pin. "Sorry. Here you are." Cissy looked down the front of her new dress, with its small yellow roses against a rich cocoa background. "You sure you ain't going to miss this dress?"

"I have plenty more. And if the only way to clothe you properly is to give up one of my own dresses, I can bear the sacrifice."

"It sure is pretty."

"I'll leave lots of fabric in the tucks down the front and back. In case you grow, if you know what I mean." Vera winked, and pulled the material tight around Cissy's chest. "Well, at least we got you a brassiere, so you aren't running around looking like the wild child of Borneo." She pinned the hem, stepping back to see if it was straight, then bent back down and repinned the front. "How often does your mother beat you like that, Cissy?"

There was no reason not to talk about it. It wasn't a secret anymore. But Cissy felt ashamed. "Only sometimes. Usually when I deserve it."

"Nobody deserves that."

"Jonas stops it sometimes. But sometimes, he gets afraid."

Vera stood up. "Next time she does that, you run, Cissy. You run like hell and don't look back. What she's doing is wrong. You do not ever deserve that. And Jonas is just a little boy, really."

"I think something *is* wrong with me, Aunt Vera. Ma ain't mean to anyone but me." Cissy felt jumbled inside. She felt she stood on an island by herself, different from Vera, different from Jonas, different from every other soul who'd ever crossed her path. Her island was called The Island Where Nothing You Do Is Right. She continued, "I try so hard. I do exactly what she says, but it ain't exactly right." Cissy shook her head. She didn't want to talk about it anymore. She wanted to think about the social and dancing with Rusty Tarns. It was too close, too raw. It reminded her of all the places she still ached, both inside and out. "What time's Mack picking us up tomorrow?"

"Seven o'clock. How's it feel around the waist?"

"Too tight."

"I wish Rose would come with us," Vera said. "It'd be good for her to go out. See her friends."

"Ouch! Watch what you're doing."

"Sorry."

"Vera?"

"Hmm?"

"How long you staying with us?" Cissy asked.
"Why?"

"Don't know. Just wondered." Vera let out a seam, and Cissy took the chance for a quick breath. "Maybe you could marry Mack, and then you could live here always."

"It's just a social, Cissy."

"You sure? Maybe he likes you."

"I'm sure."

"One hundred percent, absolutely, without-a-doubt sure?"

"Nothing's ever one hundred percent, without-a-doubt, absolute," Vera said.

"So are you staying on with us? You must have lots of friends who miss you in Denver."

Vera's hand trembled as she pulled in the waist of the dress.

"Daddy probably misses you, too," Cissy said.

"*Frank*. If there ever was a man thought he was God, it would be my brother." Vera sighed and moved over to the bureau. "You understand love, Cissy?"

Cissy thought, *Of course I do*. She looked right at Aunt Vera and knew exactly what love meant.

Vera's eyes focused on William Powell's martini in the *Thin Man* lobby card. "Grown-ups sometimes love the wrong people. Or the wrong person loves us and everything goes topsy-turvy until you think it's all right to be walking around on your head all day. But you can't help who you love, can you?" Vera's mouth turned up on one side. "Like I can't help but love you." Vera now beamed. "Hop on down, honey. No need to spread heartache around. Let's find Rose and get her approval on this."

"It's fine. I like the dress just like this."

"With all the pins in it? You know I promised her. Come on."

In the kitchen, Ma wiped flour from her hands, then circled around Cissy, picking at the shoulders, pulling at the waist. "Are you sure it's not too short, Vera?"

"It's what all the girls are wearing. You should get to town more and see the fashions these days."

"Mmm-hmm."

"She looks beautiful, doesn't she? Like a real young lady."

"I wouldn't say beautiful," Ma said. "No, I would definitely not say that."

"You should get your eyes checked, then," Vera said sharply.

"It's too . . ." Ma pursed her mouth. "No."

Cissy swallowed. Why was Ma always so contrary to things?

"Rose, it's fine," Vera said. "She'll be the belle of the ball."

"What would you know about it?" Ma asked.

Vera looked directly at her sister-in-law, not even so much as blinking. "I know," she said, "what I know. And I know Cissy should wear this dress."

"She looks too grown-up. I'm afraid—"

"The dress is fine, Rose."

"But—"

"It's fine."

"Turn around," Ma said to Cissy. "All right. But if I hear one word from someone about Cissy looking loose in that dress, I will personally cut it up myself." Giving Vera a look of resignation, she left the room.

Cissy flew to Vera, hugging her as tightly as the pins in the dress would allow. "You did it. You did it!"

"It's just a dress, Cissy."

"I can't believe she said yes. You just told her 'Rose, she's wearing this dress,' and that's the end of it."

"I didn't do anything, honey."

"Yes, you did. You don't even know."

Chapter Ten

Cissy turned in front of Ma's long mirror. A real grown-up dress. She stuck out her hip, as she'd seen Vera do, barely recognizing herself. "Why, if I was to catch myself walking down the street, I'd say I was pretty."

She patted the picture of Daddy pinned to the inside of the new dress. Right next to her heart, where it belonged.

Vera swept into the room, glorious in royal blue, her black curls a halo around her head. Cissy didn't think she had ever seen anyone so beautiful in all her life.

"Mack's here, honey," Vera said. "Pinch your cheeks for some color."

"And how is your mother these days?" Dotty loved to poke her beak in places she didn't belong.

Cissy thought someone must have spiked her

Coca-Cola, so woozy was she with people leaning in close to her to be heard above the fiddle, banjo, and guitar. All she saw were lips: wide and flabby, thin and cautious, fluttery, almost blue. People loved bad news, and Rose Funk was the best bad news around.

Cissy, ready to crack her soda bottle over the head of the next snoop, hunkered into the shadows at the end of the long wooden table, and watched Vera and Mack dance.

She swiped at a fly that kept landing on the lip of the bottle and felt the wood floor shaking beneath her from the stomps of the dancers. Puffs of air blew through the open-sided tent, bringing the sound of dark mumbles of the men drinking out beyond the bend of the creek.

She looked around for Jonas. He was nowhere in sight. She figured he was probably off with Lucille somewhere.

A freckled hand thumped the table, and Cissy grabbed her Coke to steady it.

"Well, hey there, Cissy Funk." Rusty Tarns squeezed in close, although there were ten feet of empty bench on either side.

His red hair was slicked back so tightly against his head, it looked like it had popped his ears right out. She tried not to stare, but those ears rivaled Clark Gable's. She took a sip of her soda and swayed along with the "Tennessee Waltz."

"I said, hey there." Rusty sidled in closer.

"Hey, yourself." She hoped her voice didn't sound as fluttery as it felt. She loved his sweet green eyes. She'd known Rusty all her life, and those eyes had always made her heart do a little flip.

"You look good there, Cissy." He rolled his eyes and stared at her chest.

She crossed her arms. "You keep your eyes where they belong Rusty, or I'll have my brother pull them out of your head."

"Aw, hooey. You want to dance?"

She looked at his freshly scrubbed hands with the black-edged crescent moon nails, traced with grease from working on his father's tractor for years. She put her hand in his.

They cut in to the group, and he grabbed her too tightly around the waist. She stomped on his toe to get him to loosen up. Vera swung by and pinched her cheek, giggling in a way that told Cissy she'd had a few drinks.

Every place Rusty touched brought little prickles to Cissy's skin. A strange feeling she half wanted to itch and half wanted to prickle more. Rusty smiled his wide Tarns smile. He'd been sweet on her in school; he'd even walked her home a few times.

"How's Ray Jr.?" she asked, just for a topic.

"He's coming later. With Lucille."

Cissy leaned back on his arm. "With who?"

"*Lucille*. Ray's asking her to marry him."

"Lucille?! Lucille and *Ray*?" Cissy asked. "Since

when? When's he asking her to marry him?"

"Tonight."

"She can't! I mean, they're too young to get married. Ray's only seventeen."

"That's old enough."

The banjo rolls became faster as the song changed. Cissy disentangled herself from Rusty's arms, and pushed through the crowd.

"Don't you want another dance?" Rusty called out.

"Not now. I have to go find Jonas." Cissy stepped off the wood floor onto the hard dirt, then turned toward the creek. She had to warn Jonas.

She smelled the cigarette smoke before she got there, and as her eyes adjusted to the dark, she made out groups of men sitting against tree trunks, passing bottles. No Jonas, though. Big Jake stepped out in front of her, his barrel chest all the larger in a white shirt and vest. No doubt he'd supplied all this hooch from his bar.

"I think you lost your way, girlie," Jake said.

"I'm looking for my brother."

"I haven't seen him. You seen him, Merle? Joe? No one's seen him. A pretty little girl like you shouldn't be leaving the dance all alone."

A few men chuckled; Big Jake laughed out loud. Cissy turned away, feeling threatened by the crooked smiles and heavy breath of the men.

Jake laid his hand on her shoulder and spun her

around. "How about a little kiss, pretty little girl?"

His thick lips landed squarely on hers, and she felt his teeth against her mouth, and his hand grabbing her breast. She pulled away from him. "I'm gonna tell Dotty you did that."

Jake stuck a thumb in his waistband. "Go ahead. It was just a friendly peck, that's all." He licked his lips and glanced at the other men.

"That wasn't a little peck."

"And who's to say different?" He leaned toward her, his whiskey breath hot on her cheek. "Not you, little girl."

Cissy's heart pounded against her chest. "Goddamn you, Jake," she hissed. She spit right in his face, then turned and ran.

She stumbled away, grabbing at a tree to keep her balance. She could hear the men laughing behind her. Skirting along the edge of the creek bed, she followed the glimmering white lights strung along the white tent top. Back inside, she slid into her seat, wiping her mouth, but still tasting Jake's lips on hers like an indelible mark. Could everyone look at her and see what had happened?

The Hasty twins squinted at her from the next table and whispered to Dotty. Dotty swatted a fly away from her nose and cut a look at Cissy. Then she smiled and waved.

They didn't know. And she wouldn't tell. No one

would believe her. So she swallowed her secret, letting it sink to the pit of her stomach. She stepped back on her island. If she hadn't gone down by the creek, Big Jake wouldn't have put his sticky lips on hers. If she hadn't danced with Rusty, hadn't heard about Lucille, she wouldn't have thought of the creek to begin with. Always, always wrong.

Vera plopped down next to Cissy, her face flushed from dancing. She readjusted the red ostrich feather hanging limply from her hat. "You having fun, honey? I saw you dancing with Rusty. He's going to be a looker, mark my words." She winked, then yelled out toward the band. "How about some jazz, fellas? You like jazz, Cissy? Low, hot jazz. That'll make you dance. You'd think we were in Alabama or Tennessee, with all this fiddling."

"I ain't feeling so good, Aunt Vera. Can we go home?"

"Someday, child, I'm going to take you to the big city and you're going to see the whole world light up before you. And we're going to go out on the town and hear real jaaazzz." The word became a slice of its own music. "You don't know, but I am a wild, wild woman." Vera's eyes flashed, and her nostrils flared. "There's a club in Denver, has the most amazing singer—"

"How are the two most beautiful women in the room?" Mack placed tall glasses of tea with shaved ice in front of them.

"We're having the best time," Vera said. "Isn't that the truth, Cissy?"

"You all right?" Mack asked Cissy.

Before Cissy could answer, Vera's jaw dropped open.

"What, Vera?" Cissy asked.

"Well, look what the cat drug in." Vera pointed toward Lucille on Ray Tarns, Jr.'s arm, wearing a very smug look.

Cissy clenched her fists. "I'm ready to go, Mack."

"Lord, it's hotter now than it was at noon." Vera ambled up the walk, her feet too tired to prance, and passed Ma sitting on the porch steps. "Doesn't it ever cool off around here, Rose? How about I get us lemonade." Vera banged the screen door, and her steps faded to the back of the house.

Mack wiped at his neck with a handkerchief. "Cissy doesn't feel too well, so we brought her on home, Rose."

"What happened, Cissy?" Ma asked.

"Nothing. Tired, that's all."

"Come here, child." Ma held Cissy's chin, staring at her with those cat eyes. "Where's Jonas?" She looked worried.

Cissy turned away. Jonas was the shining boy. Jonas—who was probably getting his heart broke somewhere—was all that worried Ma. If only she

78

could tell Ma what had happened to her. But Ma wouldn't believe her. Ma would blame her for what Big Jake did.

"Ah, hear the music?" Mack said. In the stillness and the heat, the soft sounds of the fiddle at the dance floated in the air.

Cissy sidled up the porch stairs and sat on the bench by the door. She glared out of the darkness at her mother. Ma didn't care what had happened to her.

"How about a dance, Rose?" Mack asked.

Ma looked at him with a mixture of surprise and hesitation. "Well, I'm not sure . . ."

"Just one."

"All right."

Before they could move off the porch, Vera pushed open the screen door. "Drinks for all!"

The three adults sat on the steps, and as the breeze shifted, the fiddle was lost in the steady pulse of crickets.

"I have a bad feeling about Jonas," Ma said.

"It's probably gas." Vera chortled, then put her hand over her mouth.

"Who cares about Jonas?" Cissy blurted out.

"You still here, honey?" Vera shaded her eyes and scanned the porch. "Why are you hiding in the shadows? Come on out here."

Cissy leaned further back in the dark. She'd wait until Ma went to bed, then tell Vera what happened.

Vera would understand. Vera might even march on down to Jake's and give him an earful.

"Cissy has a beau," Vera said. "And a damn good looker he is, too. It's on account of the new dress, you know. Made Cissy the prettiest girl there."

The dress. Cissy bunched the dress in her hands, trying to crush it. She wanted to rip it off, to tear it into small pieces she could throw to the wind. She didn't want to be the prettiest girl, she didn't want any attention. The dress brought on Rusty's rolling eyes. And big, ugly Jake.

Vera didn't understand. And if what Big Jake did was what Rusty would do, then Cissy thought she'd like to freeze herself in time. She didn't want what the dress or growing up brought with them. It was dirty, and it made her feel sick.

She ran into the house, tugging the thin fabric of the dress over her head. She threw the dress into a corner and pulled on her dungarees and big shirt. Her teeth chattered. She held herself tightly around her chest, trying to hold in a rage that felt like it would shatter her bones. There was no one to trust, and everyone was out to hurt her. Lucille, and Jake, and Ma. And even Vera, who tried to dress her like a little adult.

A sob welled up inside her. She wanted Daddy. She wanted to sit on his lap and have his arms protect her from the world. She wanted him to keep out the hurt.

Chapter Eleven

Cissy pulled a carrot out of the ground. The morning heat was unbearable. The earth sizzled around the carrot, as if it might burst into a ball of flame. She stretched her back and leaned against the house, thankful for the small amount of shade it offered. Ma paddled the rag rug strung on the clothing line, raising a cloud of dust. She reminded Cissy of a wind-up toy.

Jonas hadn't come home after the social. Ma had roused Cissy at dawn, and kept her busy, the constant motion of household chores and tending the garden buffering them both against their fears. Cissy remembered all the times Jonas had said he wanted to leave. How he stayed for her, scared of what would happen if she was left alone with Ma.

She wished she'd been invited to church with Aunt Vera and Mack. She would have liked to go, to sit in the cool of the dark church, to be lulled into sleep by the drone of the minister's words.

"Don't laze around," Ma called out. "You pick those vegetables before the sun kills them all."

Cissy pulled at another carrot, but the greens broke off in her hand, leaving the bright orange top of the carrot moored in the hard ground. She stood and reached for a hoe, and saw Jonas push open the gate. His shirt was splotched with dirt and blood, one eye bruised and swollen shut. He weaved toward Ma.

"Jonas!" The wooden paddle dangled at Ma's side. "What in God's name happened to you?"

Jonas touched his lip with the tip of his tongue. His one good eye slid to the side, then snapped back forward. "Get out of my way."

"You answer me."

"I'm only here to collect my things," he said.

Ma grabbed at his sleeve. "You're not going anywhere. You scared me to death, Jonas. You owe me an explanation."

He shook his head and jerked away, taking the porch steps two at a time, stumbling at the top.

Ma stayed right with him, and held her arm in front of the screen door. "Don't walk away from me. Tell me what happened."

Cissy crouched near the porch, peeking over its edge.

Jonas spun toward Ma. "Don't you know? Ain't you had a *vision*?"

"Just talk to me—"

"I don't want to talk to you! I don't ever want to talk to you again." He pushed her up against the wall. "You stupid . . . I was supposed to marry Lucille. She was all I wanted, Ma. And it's your fault. Your fault. Everybody knows you're crazy. Nobody wants to hang around a crazy family. You and your visions. You and your hate. Why, Ma?" Burying his head in her chest, he pulled in ragged, wheezing breaths. Then he pushed her aside and slammed into the house.

Ma put her hand to her mouth and bent over. Her silent scream pierced Cissy's being. She looked down at Cissy. "Don't look at me. Don't *look* at me."

Cissy scrambled away from Ma, ran through the back door, and bounded up the steps to Jonas's room. "Don't, Jonas. You can't do this. You can't leave me here."

"I got to go, Cissy." He wadded up a shirt and stuffed it into his pillowcase. "I need your money. What you got hidden?"

"But that's—"

"I'll get it myself."

Cissy followed him down the steps to the living room. He picked up her photo, cracked it across the end table, then picked the coins out of the shattered glass on the floor and pocketed them. "I'll pay you back." He stopped moving to look at her. "You've got Vera, now."

"But she might leave. What do I do then? Jonas—"

"I'm sorry."

"Please stay."

"Look, I'll send you money. Then you can come out and we'll . . ." He swallowed the rest of his words. He held out a hand, then let it drop to his side. "I'm so sorry."

He walked over and grabbed Cissy, pulling her close. She felt the pounding of his heart against hers. She breathed in his sweet smell—still sweet, even through the sweat and blood and sorrow. She would never, never forget it.

"You stay strong, Cissy."

"I love you, Jonas."

"I love you, too," he said. "I got to go."

And, just as Cissy had imagined and feared it, Jonas walked out onto the plains, until he was a dark spot on the flat horizon.

She knelt to pick up the shards of glass, and sensed her mother's cold shadow. A great shiver passed down Cissy's body.

"He left?" Ma asked.

"Yes, ma'am."

Ma nodded, then went into her bedroom and quietly shut the door.

∞ ∞ ∞

Jonas's absence hung heavy in the corners of the house, and Cissy could not bear it. She walked outside, but even the broad sky seemed heavy. A numbness filled her, the same deadening she had felt when Daddy left.

She remembered the note. A single note scratched on the back of the milk bill the day after Violet's funeral. *Will send money*, Daddy's familiar handwriting said. Nothing else. Then Aunt Vera came, and Ma was sent away for a few weeks. Somewhere. Somewhere so bad, she came home with an empty stare and a shock of gray hair running like molten silver through the red.

Cissy trudged over to the rag rug hanging in the yard. Better not to remember. Better to ignore the stone that sat on her heart. A mass that might drag her down under the earth. Jonas had been her best friend. How do you live without one half of who you are? She took the rug inside, then moved the easy chair so it covered the worn spot as she'd seen Ma do a hundred times. She replaced her photo of Douglas Fairbanks, Jr., in its now empty frame, smoothing down the rip along his chin and cheek. She cut newspaper into small squares, then set the papers on the outhouse shelf. She scooped out chicken feed, she scooped up eggs, she cleaned the henhouse, she raked the dirt yard. Cissy almost convinced herself that today was the same as yesterday.

Mack brought Vera home from church, and then drove away.

Vera looked out over the sun-covered brown fields and frowned. "Is there ever any relief from this heat?"

Cissy put her hands in the pockets of her dungarees and rocked back on her heels. "Jonas left."

"What?"

"I said Jonas left."

"He left home? Where'd he go?"

Cissy shrugged. "He's just gone. And I think it's for good."

Vera covered her mouth with her hand. "Oh, Lord. Your ma must be . . ." She ran up to the house. "Rose? Rose!"

And Cissy thought, *Now I am alone.*

Chapter Twelve

Ma took to sitting on the porch, knees curled to her chin, as she had when Daddy left so many months before. Sitting and staring, no movement, no sound, just watchful eyes. Her body seemed to fade, and sometimes when Cissy walked by, she mistook Ma for a shadow.

Why couldn't Ma see that, even though she no longer had Jonas, she still had Cissy? Cissy wanted Ma to do something, anything. Anything was better than the deadness surrounding her like a shroud. It was like when Violet died. Cissy hadn't been enough then either, and she wasn't enough now.

Three days after Jonas left, Vera snapped her purse shut and said, "I have to get out of this house. We're going to get you a haircut, Cissy."

On the way to town, Cissy asked, "What's going

to happen now, Aunt Vera?"

"We're getting you a haircut, that's what's going to happen."

"Ma's worse than before. I'm scared."

Vera spun on her heel and held Cissy's shoulders. "Nothing's going to happen. I'm here. And I've made Rose promise to leave you alone. Have I let you down yet?"

"I love you, Aunt Vera."

"I know you do, honey. I told you I'd take care of things. I never break my word."

Once they reached town, Vera stepped into the Hasty's to buy some pork chops and Cissy crossed over to the Odeon. The theater was open only on Thursdays, Fridays, and Saturdays, but Mack might be in his apartment upstairs.

"Hey, Cissy."

Rusty Tarns's voice made Cissy jump. He held a small box covered by an old towel.

"What's in there?" Cissy asked.

"A pup." He set the box down on the sidewalk and pulled back the towel to show Cissy a small little puppy, chocolate brown from his nose to his big eyes to the end of his long tail. "I just got this one left. Pa drowned the other two. I rescued this one just in time." Cissy knelt down and reached for the puppy.

She held the puppy to her face, breathing in

its dusty scent. It squirmed around in her hands, then gave her a tiny lick on the nose. Cissy kissed the top of his head. "If you was mine, I'd call you Fairbanks."

"Take him. I can't keep him."

"Really? I can have him?" She held the puppy close to her face. "Fairbanks. Oh, Rusty, he's so cute!"

"You know, Lucille's tore up about Jonas leaving."

Cissy's throat tightened. "She should have thought of that before."

"The way I heard it, her dad set up the whole thing. He made her think Jonas was no good. Nothing but trouble. You know how Mr. Mason is. Kind of thinks your ma's a bit, well . . ." Rusty twirled a finger at his temple and crossed his eyes. "Said he didn't want that in the family. But I think that's a crock."

Cissy looked up at Rusty's shy smile, then ran her hands over Fairbanks's back to keep them from shaking.

Rusty knelt down next to her. "You all right?"

Cissy needed to talk. To talk it all out, to somebody who would listen without interrupting or judging. She lowered her voice, so no one passing would overhear her. "When Violet died, Ma just lay in bed holding her. A dead baby. Just lay there for hours, squeezing Violet to her chest. She loved Violet. Loved her best of all of us. But I hate Violet. I wish she'd never been born and never died. It's all her fault. She's what turned my ma into something different. And there ain't nothing I can do to make it right. Every time I try, it turns out worse than if I'd left it be." She didn't mention how Ma took swipes at her; that hurt had wound its way down deep in Cissy's darkness, and she never wanted anyone else to know about it. "Sometimes, I feel I live on my own island. It's all rocky and there ain't no trees or grass. I can see you and I can see everyone way in the distance. I'm lonely and safe all at the same time." She sighed. "If I could, I'd live with Vera or Mack, watch the pictures all day long, and drink grape NEHIs till I was sick. And get off my island. You probably think I'm nuts, now."

Then—quick, and sweet, and soft—Rusty grazed Cissy's cheek with his lips. He was off like a shot, leaving her sitting in the full sun with a round puppy on her lap.

She couldn't move; didn't want to move. The world had just broadened and she with it. At the same time, everything felt as tiny as the fiery spot of skin Rusty's lips had touched.

This wasn't anything like Big Jake; she didn't feel dirty at all. She suddenly became separate from her old being, and a floating sensation pulled her to her feet. She was no longer Ma's daughter, no longer a little girl. She was Cissy Funk, grown and bold. She shook her head. All because of a little kiss.

Dear Beth,

It HAPPENED. I've been kissed before you, so I win the bet!!! Rusty just leaned over, for no reason at all, and there it was. I can't tell you how my brain is spinning. I want to run over and see him right now, except it's the middle of the night! I have passed the threshold to womanhood, so you better hurry up and join me.

And he gave me a puppy, Beth. A roly-poly little brown thing. I called him Fairbanks after our very favorite movie star. He's curled up on my lap right now, which is why my handwriting looks so sloppy.

Dotty cut all my hair off. I look a little boyish, but more grown-up, too.

Jonas left, under catastrophic circumstances, and you know how Ma dotes on Jonas. Lucille's going to marry Ray Tarns, only I don't think she wants to. Oh, no! I just thought of something—if I marry Rusty, than Lucille would be my <u>sister-in-law</u>. I'll have to think this through carefully, because that thought could make me sick. Of course, if she just married Jonas, and I didn't marry

Rusty, we'd be sisters, anyway. Stupid Lucille must be my cross to bear!

Beth, I wish you'd write me, so I know you're well.

Yours always,
Narcissus

Chapter Thirteen

It had been two weeks since Jonas left. No one talked about him. No one could. Cissy felt a flutter of guilt that she thought more about Rusty than she did about her brother. It had been days since she even thought about Daddy. Guilt-ridden, she began to pin photos of him to her dress, and she made sure to look at them each morning when she cleaned the henhouse.

While she had to make an effort to remember Daddy, she had no difficulty remembering Rusty's lips. She wondered when she would see him again, and hoped he might stop by. At night she stared out Jonas's window, watching the yellow lights in the Tarns house, and could sleep only when they blinked out.

Cissy felt she was about to turn a corner, that soon she would leave behind her old self, step around the bend, and become . . . what? She cried, feeling she had lost all that was familiar, terrified of the unknown. Maybe Jonas had turned the corner too. Maybe that was why he left. He'd been brave enough to make the turn. Cissy wondered if she could ever be so bold herself.

A letter came from Jonas. Ma practically ripped the thin paper. She handed it to Vera to read.

Vera cleared her throat, sat on the couch, and read, "'Dear folks, I got a job in Kansas City, now, working on cars. It's swell here. Real pretty. Lots of cornfields. How's things there? Is Vera still there? How's my little sis? You take care of yourself, Ma. Love, Jonas.'"

Ma snatched back the letter. "That's it?"

"He's all right," Vera said. "Isn't that enough?"

Ma's face paled, and she slumped into the easy chair. She crumpled the letter, then put her face against her fists.

"Oh, Ma," Cissy said. She folded her arms around her mother. She needed, just this once, to feel that Ma was like she used to be. A mother who cared and comforted and made the world all right.

"Get away from me." Ma jerked Cissy's arms off her.

Cissy stepped back. A fury inside her grew, as if lodged in a glass bottle running from her gut to her throat. A bottle ready to crack from its fullness, ready to explode shards of glass throughout her organs. She imagined pieces piercing her lung, cutting open her heart, slicing the skin near her belly. She pulled her arm back to strike, then stopped. If she hit Ma—like she wanted to do with every strand of every muscle—she would be like Ma. Just like Ma. She shook with the pain of holding that arm back. It would be so easy to let loose. It would be a relief. It would be a reach across that rocky island and a chance to say "I am here, too." Letting her hand fly would mean turning the corner and becoming someone new.

No. Becoming Ma.

She dropped her arm. She vowed she would never become Ma.

But also around that corner was strength. Cissy grabbed it with all her might.

Chapter Fourteen

The next morning, Fairbanks wiggled his way over to where Ma sat on the porch step, plopping his front paws on her lap. He jumped up and licked her cheeks and nose and eyelids.

"That dog should be tied up. He'll get into the chickens, otherwise."

That's *my* dog, Cissy thought. She scooped him up, not wanting to share him. "Leave Ma alone." She held him tight so he couldn't wriggle back to Ma. Cissy stepped directly in front of Ma. "I know you miss Jonas, Ma, but *I'm* here."

Ma's vacant eyes didn't respond.

Cissy set Fairbanks down. "Get up, Ma. There ain't nothing to look at on the road. Jonas ain't coming back. But I'm right here." Cissy glared down at her mother. She felt reckless and angry, still filled with bitterness from the night before. "Had one of your visions? See something in the chicken shit in the yard?"

Ma's eyes locked on Cissy. The corner of her mouth curled up in a smirk, and challenge shivered down her body. Cissy took a step backward.

"Keep that dog away from the chickens," Ma said.

"You're just gonna sit out here and rot, aren't you?" Cissy spit out. "Sit out here like a crazy lady. That's why you ain't got any friends."

"Cissy!" Vera broke in. "What's gotten into you?"

Cissy grinned, hoping it looked innocent. "Just having a little conversation."

Vera followed Cissy into the kitchen. "Leave your mother alone. You don't know what she's gone through lately."

"I don't? Don't seem any different than the whole last year." She hated when Vera defended Ma. She set Fairbanks on a chair, wiped her hands, and put the last piece of pie on a plate. "You want to split it?"

"I'm not hungry."

"I was talking to the dog," Cissy said.

Fairbanks cocked his head, and his long ear flopped on the table.

Vera's frowning eyebrows made one long line of black across her forehead. "Put that dog down." Her fingers drummed the countertop. "I know you're upset, honey."

Cissy drew in a breath. "Whatever about?"

"Whatever about? Why, most likely everything."

"I ain't upset."

"I'm *not* upset," Vera muttered.

"What's the difference, Aunt Vera? Not, ain't—who cares?"

Vera wiped her brow and mumbled, "It's too hot for this." She gestured toward Fairbanks. "And I'm asking you to please put that dog on the floor."

"Why?"

"Because I said so."

"You ain't my ma," Cissy said, surprised by her own words. She set a hunk of pie in front of the puppy, then dug a fork into her own piece.

Vera rubbed her eyebrows. "You're being contrary. *Contrary.* And childish."

"Why are you here, anyway, Aunt Vera? You ain't never said."

Vera opened her mouth, then shut it quick like a fish gasping for air. "Let's talk about something else," Vera said.

"Must've been something bad."

"No, it was *not* bad. Not at all. I just wanted to see you."

"That's why you brought everything you owned? Did you lose your job?" Cissy licked her lips. "I'm not a child. You can tell me."

"Mmm."

"I ain't. I've been kissed, so there."

"Oh, have you?" Vera asked.

Cissy peered down at her hands resting in her lap.

"So now you feel you're a big grown-up adult?" Vera shook her head. "Who kissed you? Rusty Tarns?"

"That's none of your business."

Vera sat down. "Well, your blush just gave me the answer. You be careful with boys, Cissy. Why, just touching one could cause you all sorts of misery. And you know what I mean by that."

Cissy pushed out her lips and lied. "Of course I know. I read all about it in the encyclopedia."

Cissy pulled Fairbanks onto her lap. She checked behind his ears for ticks. She raised his head and checked under his neck. She pulled a burr from the dog's left front paw.

"You promise you just kissed him?"

Cissy shrugged.

"You don't do anything else until you're married, you understand? Then, of course, you can get closer. . . . You know about the birds and the bees, Cissy?"

Ma darted into the kitchen. "What are you telling her? What dirt are you *telling* her?" She slapped Vera.

Vera held a hand up to her cheek. "Jesus, Rose—"

"I'm her mother. *I am!* You remember that, Vera."

Cissy watched the vein pop out on Ma's jaw. She slid out of her chair and backed toward the kitchen door.

"You come in my house and fill my children's heads with nonsense," Ma said. "It's your fault Jonas left, and I'll never forgive you for that! Never!"

Vera circled around the table, keeping it between her and Rose. "It's not my fault he left. I never gave Jonas any ideas—"

"You don't have to *talk*, Vera, to spread your filth. You've rolled around in the mud so long, you stink from a mile away. You're not going to rub your ways on Cissy."

"What ways are those, Rose? Giving her attention? Actually giving a good goddamn what she thinks about? It's obvious you don't. Even though you are her mother."

Ma set her fists on the table and leaned toward Vera. "You listen to me, Vera, I let you come back here and share my home because I'm a charitable woman."

"That's a laugh," Vera said.

"You act like you're better than everyone around."

"No, I don't."

"Just remember, Vera, I *know* you. So don't think you're so la-de-da special. And don't you forget what I've done for you, and don't you judge me." Ma wiped her mouth with the back of her hand as if to keep back words too dark to speak. "I *know* you."

"How dare you, Rose—"

Cissy switched her weight from one foot to another, and a floorboard squeaked. Then the bottle, straining and full inside of her, burst. "Shut up! Both of you shut up!"

"Shut up? Did I hear you right?" Ma said. "Don't you ever tell me to shut up."

Cissy locked her gaze into Ma's. "I hate you."

Ma's face grew ugly and black. She put a hand around Cissy's neck and started to squeeze down.

"You are not my ma," Cissy said. She closed her eyes and repeated it over and over. "You are not my ma. You are not my ma . . ."

Ma let go and glared at Vera. "You turn everyone on me. Get out of my house."

Chapter Fifteen

In the dark early morning, Vera stuffed her dresses into the suitcase laying open on the bed. "Get those perfumes, honey, and my makeup."

Cissy reached to the counter, and accidentally knocked the spray bottle of gardenia to the floor.

"Shh, shh, shh!"

"All right already," Cissy whispered. "It's dark, you know. You could turn on a light."

"Just put the things in the case." Vera turned in a circle, patting her hand against the side of her cheek. "Now, how do we get out?"

"Jonas's window," Cissy said.

"We're going to jump? Off the roof?"

"It's okay. It's real low to the ground there."

Vera buckled the suitcase, took it by the handle, and slowly opened the door. Then she drew a deep breath. "You ready?"

Ready? Of course she wasn't. But she nodded anyway. "Oh, wait a minute." Cissy slid her hand under the wardrobe and grasped the tin box. Then she reached over the bed and pulled down the lobby card of *Little Women*. "I want to take these with me."

They tiptoed across the hall. Cissy pushed up the window in Jonas's room. "Give me the suitcase." She flung it, and covered her ears when it landed with a hard thud on the dirt below.

Vera froze, waiting for any noise from the floor below. Satisfied Ma hadn't awakened, she gestured for Cissy to crawl through the window.

Cissy twisted her leg over the sill, and her hem caught on a loose nail. She freed the material and stepped onto the roof. Why did Vera insist she wear a dress for traveling? Dungarees would have been so much easier. She dropped over the edge, hesitating before letting go of the gutter, afraid she might fall forever through the oily dark sky. But she landed softly and steadied Vera's flailing legs over the edge. She pulled off Vera's high heels a split second before Vera dropped to the ground. Holding the shoes out to Vera, she rolled her eyes. "Want to break your leg?"

Vera retrieved the suitcase. They jogged across the yard. The rusty gate creaked, and Fairbanks howled, straining against the rope that held him tied to the side of the house.

"I need to get Fairbanks," Cissy whispered.

"No. Absolutely no dog."

"But, I—"

"Leave your mother something."

"I left the note on the kitchen table. It's enough. I want my dog. I won't leave without him. She won't treat him right."

"I'm sorry, honey. We can't." Vera's eyes were firm.

Cissy ran over to Fairbanks and wrapped her arms around his neck. She buried her face in his soft fur. "I got to go, pal. You take care of Ma, all right?"

He whined quietly, and ran a warm tongue along her cheek.

The light snapped on in Ma's room.

"Oh, my God, Vera," Cissy said, "run!"

The moonless night pulled Cissy forward with hope, and the light in her mother's room pushed her with fear. Escape, her feet pounded out. Escape, escape, escape.

"Tell Rusty to look in on Fairbanks—and you look in on Ma, okay?"

Mack nodded to Cissy, handed Vera ten dollars, and then waved as the 6:33 A.M. bus for Denver pulled away from the Coronado.

Cissy rested her head against the seat and forced her eyes forward. She wouldn't look back at

Mack's troubled face, the ugly squareness of the new post office, the turn by the cemetery that meant the road home. She crossed her arms tightly and watched the magenta sunrise steal across broken fields waiting for winter wheat.

Vera patted Cissy's thigh and gave her a too-big smile. "Isn't this fun, honey?"

Cissy knew it wasn't fun. It was scary as hell. She already missed Fairbanks, and the thought of him made tears well up in her eyes. How'd Vera talk her into this, anyway?

Vera carefully applied another layer of lipstick, then pressed a tissue between her lips. She folded the tissue and placed it back in her bag.

The sun hit the corner of Cissy's tin. *Daddy,* she thought. *I'm going to see Daddy.* And excitement rose in her throat. Maybe Vera was right. Just maybe this was for the best. But Ma's pale face floated before her eyes, and she shut her lids tight against the sadness she saw. How would Ma manage alone?

Vera had to be right. Cissy slid her hand into her aunt's, and squeezed tight. This was the turn of the corner, the leap off the island. Cissy was on her way to becoming someone new.

PART TWO
DENVER, COLORADO

Chapter Sixteen

In the parking lot of the Red Rooster Diner, Cissy stretched her legs and jumped up and down. She rotated her arms like a propeller, then wrinkled her nose. "Stinks here, doesn't it?"

The bus driver snorted. "Greeley. Some days I've got to wear a bandanna to keep out the smell of the meatpacking plants."

The wind blew little curlicues of dirt across the lot and highway. Cissy turned toward the restaurant. What was taking Vera so long?

A car drove by, and Cissy coughed from the dust that spewed in her face. Straddling a fence post, she kept the sun at her back and the dark jagged line of the mountains in view. It was a brand-new world. Anything could happen. Never mind the niggling of guilt she felt in the back of her throat for leaving Ma. No, never mind. Cissy would live with Daddy and Aunt Vera. They might even have school still going in Denver, and she would make new friends—best friends, as good as or better than Beth. And she wouldn't be afraid of anything.

Vera strolled out of the cafe with a newspaper rolled in her hands. "What are you doing?"

Cissy jumped off the fence. "Looking at the silver lining."

Vera climbed the bus stairs and swung into her seat. She dabbed at the corner of her eye with a handkerchief.

Cissy sat beside her. "Why're you crying, Aunt Vera?"

Vera sniffed, folded her handkerchief in thirds, and dropped it in her purse. "I'm not crying. It's the dust, that's all."

Cissy lay her head on her aunt's shoulder. "We did the right thing, didn't we?"

Vera sighed and looked out the bus window. "I hope so, honey. I truly do."

"Hey!" Vera shook Cissy awake. "Take a look ahead."

Cissy peered through the grimy streaks on the bus's windshield. Just to make sure she was seeing things right, she rubbed her eyes. A city of light rose like a phoenix from the yellow plains.

Cissy grabbed her chest before her heart could fly right out of it. The weary stretch of fields actually ended; she hadn't thought it possible. Yet here was the evidence, right in front of her. And somewhere in the magnificent Denver skyline, Daddy waited for her. "Holy mackerel!"

"We're almost there," Vera said. "Wait'll you see the capitol. And Elitch's. Why there's a bandstand and a theater, and it's just something else!"

Cissy nodded.

"And honey, the movies you can see! Of course, we'll have to deal with your father." Vera patted Cissy's knee. "But you leave Frank to me."

Outside the bus station, the shocking racket of voices, the metallic clang of trolley cars, the tires screeching into cement bombarded Cissy's ears. Loaded down with baggage, Vera and Cissy wove through the crowds.

Young boys selling apples filled the block of Market between 16th and 17th. "Two cents! Fresh picked apples!" The boys yelled with determination and desperation.

The May D&F clock on its pale brick tower struck three times. Cissy jumped an oily puddle. Men stood near a gray stone church, three deep, a hundred long, waiting for a small handout of food. Their clothes sagged at the shoulders, hung loose at the belly; still, they kept their backs stiff and their hats cocked, a last vestige of dignity.

Cissy couldn't help but notice the men noticing Vera. A man with a pencil-thin mustache and greasy patches on the knees of his pants whipped off his cap. "You can take me home anytime, sister."

Vera pulled Cissy faster. "This isn't a good part of town. Quick, let's catch that trolley."

The lumbering trolley spit them out of the murkiness and straight into bright, hot sunlight. Cissy's eyes grew wide as shops, banks, restaurants, and car dealerships rolled by the window. Like the cities in moving pictures, but real life. The trolley turned down a residential street lined with green elms. Here, the houses sat barely a foot apart, all of the same brick, all one story, each with a front porch and a grassy lawn.

"How do people not get lost?" she asked Vera.

Vera's knuckles turned purple and white on the suitcase handle. "Oh, but, honey, people get lost here all the time."

Chapter Seventeen

Vera flung the suitcase through the doorway of the brick house, broadsiding Frank Funk and knocking a plate of cold chicken and coleslaw from his hands. Cissy'd never seen a whiter face than her daddy's. He staggered backward, looking for all the world like he was going to faint.

No one moved or spoke. Cissy wiped her clammy hands along her dress, and was surprised to find her legs shaking.

"What in the world—" Daddy set his fists on his hips.

"Hello, Frank." Vera squared her shoulders.

Wiping her hands on her dress once more, Cissy walked up to her father and placed her arms around his solid waist. She lay her cheek against his chest, breathing in the smell of his aftershave. A familiar smell she'd curled into for so many years. "Hey, Daddy."

"What are you doing here?" Daddy asked.

Her father's voice ran through Cissy's body, bringing tears to her eyes.

He pulled away and held Cissy at arm's length, looking at her as if trying to decide if she was real.

Was he happy or angry? He hadn't seen her in eighteen months; maybe he didn't recognize her. Maybe she was nothing more to him than some beanpole of a wayward and strange girl.

Suddenly, his gold tooth gleamed out from his smile, and he squeezed her to him. "My, my," he muttered. "Would you like a drink? I've got a bottle of Bubble-Up. Or a glass of milk, if you want it. Here, I'll, uh . . . sit down." He led Cissy by the shoulders to the sofa. "You sure have grown." He poked at her shoulder, touched the top of her head, then stuck both his hands in his pockets.

"We need to talk," Vera said.

Daddy's mouth twitched. His eyes flickered to the splash of coleslaw and chicken on the carpet. "You hungry, Cissy?"

Cissy shook her head. How could she be hungry? Finally, *finally*, Daddy stood before her, not more than two feet away. She wouldn't need her pictures anymore, wouldn't need to kiss the cool black-and-white images. Now she would see him every morning, every night. She'd wait for a kiss on the top of her head, and learn what his favorite meal was so she could cook it for him. They would play gin rummy until dawn. No, she wasn't hungry.

Daddy glared at Vera. "You should have called first, Vera."

"Why? You'd have told us not to come."

Daddy's foot scuffed heavily against the floor. "Are you just visiting or passing through?"

"We're here to stay, Daddy," Cissy said. "Here with you."

"What?"

"We don't want anything from you, Frank," Vera said. "I'll find us a place to stay, and you won't have to worry your block head that we'll be in the way."

"You are a work of art, Vera. Did Rose agree to this?"

"I have money."

"Maxine send it to you?"

"No."

"Who'd you charm it from this time?" He crossed his arms. "You can't just come waltzing in here and tell me you're moving in."

"Why not?" Cissy asked.

"Why not what?" Daddy said.

"Why can't we stay here?"

Vera slumped back on the sofa. "Cissy, your father doesn't want me here. He doesn't want—"

"Shut up, Vera." He said this like he was tired of repeating himself.

"She hit Cissy, Frank."

"What? Did your mother hit you, Cissy?"

A shame crept up Cissy's legs, winding its way

around her neck until it twisted at her throat. She shrugged.

"Did she hit you?" Daddy asked again. "You give her a reason to?"

Vera narrowed her eyes. "Cissy didn't do anything to deserve what she got from Rose."

Daddy held up a hand for silence. "Cissy? What happened between you and your mother?"

Cissy licked her lips. "I don't know."

"You don't know?"

"I just don't want to live there anymore. She don't want me, anyhow."

Vera looked down at her feet. "We just need a place for tonight, Frank. We won't put you out."

He rocked back on his heels, then paced the room, his eyes glazed with frustration.

"One night, Frank," Vera said. "Can't you see how tired she is?"

Daddy stopped midway across the living room and peered down at Cissy. "All right. One night." He took his suit coat from the dining room chair and shrugged it on. "I need a drink," he said as he went out the door.

"Only one night?" Cissy asked. "I thought I'd be able to . . . I mean . . ." She felt close to crying. The brand-new world, so full of possibilities, shrank before her.

"It'll be better this way, honey," Vera said.

Cissy didn't think so.

Chapter Eighteen

Cissy opened her eyes to the morning and, careful not to disturb Aunt Vera, sat up in the bed. For a moment, she thought she was still in a dream, in a room of pink. Then she realized she actually *was* in a room with a pink comforter and pillowcases and light-pink walls. Though she had passed out the minute her head touched the pillow, her body felt as tired as if she had been awake for a week.

Spying a tortoiseshell brush lying crossways on the vanity, she stood and picked it up. One long strand of dark hair curled in its bristles. She yanked it out, then pulled the brush through her own short hair. The face in the mirror caught her eyes. Her own. But the pieces of chin, ear, and cheek didn't add up to the face she knew so well. An edge in her dark eyes made them black as night.

Vera made a muffled sound and pulled a pillow over her head.

Cissy picked up her dress, but it was wrinkled and smelled like travel and sweat. She pulled her dungarees and Jonas's big shirt from her bag and quietly dressed.

Daddy, in an undershirt and worn trousers, sat in the small dining room reading the paper, a cup of steaming coffee in his hand.

"Morning." Cissy's mouth felt dry.

Daddy started, dropping the paper to the table. "Good morning."

Cissy slid into the chair next to him. She was at a loss for words. She'd talked to his picture so often, but now, here he was, big as day, and she couldn't think of one thing to say.

"You hungry?" Daddy said. "I could make you an egg."

"I'm okay for now."

"All right." He looked at the blue spruce outside the dining room window. His eyes grazed the headlines. He picked something out of his coffee. "The *Post* is forecasting thunderstorms later. That'll cool us off a bit."

"How's the encyclopedia business?" Cissy asked.

"Nobody reads anymore. Crying shame. Nope, I've moved on to washing machines. Everybody needs to wash their clothes. That's just one of my concerns. You've got to have a lot of irons in the fire to get ahead."

"I bet it's hard to sell washing machines when everybody's poor," Cissy said.

"Not everyone's poor. No, sir. There's a good many people who would take out a second mort-gage to own a dee-luxe electric washing machine." His salesman's voice sang. He used to read Cissy to sleep with that voice.

"I got a picture of you and Ma," Cissy said. "Want to see?"

"Sure."

She pulled the photographs from her back pocket and handed him the one where he stood by the car.

Daddy sank back against his chair. "Well, I'll be. I sure loved that old Packard."

"See?" Cissy pointed at the picture. "Ma's all in the shadows there."

"Is she?"

"She looks pretty, don't she?"

"Look at that car. I sure loved that car."

He set the photo facedown on the table. "Let me see the other one you got there."

She handed Daddy the photo she'd stolen from Vera's book, and pointed to the woman with the white-blond hair. "Who's she?"

"Where'd you get this?"

Cissy shrugged. "Aunt Vera gave it to me."

"Oh." He slid the photos back across the table, with a long look at her. "What really happened between you and your mother, Cissy?"

"Nothing."

"Don't want to talk about it, huh? How's Jonas?"

"He's in Kansas City. Got himself a job working on cars." Cissy rubbed at her nose with the back of her hand.

Daddy nodded his approval. "About time he got out in the world. Be a man. So now your mother's all alone."

The enormity of that slammed into Cissy. She hadn't put it all together until the words came out of his mouth. Ma had no one to watch over her, no one to make sure she made it through the dust storms, no one to go to town for her, or take the eggs or—but, yes, Mack would. Of course he would. Cissy had to believe he would. Mack had taken care of Cissy, saving her, saving Vera, giving them money. In fact, he always seemed to be there. Her fear eased. "Mack'll take care of her. You remember Mack, don't you, Daddy?"

Tying the belt on her yellow robe, Vera wove herself out to the dining room. She rumpled Cissy's hair, then reached down for the photos.

Cissy set her hand on top of them, trying to hide the photo she had stolen from her aunt, but Vera was too quick.

Vera looked at it, expressionless, then set the photo back down. "Any coffee?"

"Help yourself," Daddy said.

She meandered into the kitchen, then came back out with a full cup. Curling against the edge of the couch, she stared out the picture window. "Mmm. I missed that view of the mountains. There was nothing like this to look at in Ransom. Just flatness. Ad nauseam. Isn't that the truth, Cissy? What do you think of those Rocky Mountains? We'll drive up there someday. There's some beautiful lakes."

"I've circled some ads for apartments to look at," Daddy said.

"Kind of you." Vera smirked.

"And I'm taking Cissy out to the bus station."

Vera lowered her cup to the coffee table. "She's not going anywhere."

"Yeah," Cissy said. "I'm not going anywhere."

Daddy put a hand on each knee and leaned toward Cissy. "Your mother is alone out there. Family takes care of family."

"And when'd you ever do that, Frank?" Vera asked.

"I send money every month, so don't start on me. You need to take care of your ma, Cissy. You know she can't be alone."

Popping up from her seat, Cissy marched around the room, then headed straight for her father. "Why

121

can't we stay here with you? There's enough room."

"Because you can't. I'm never here."

"You're my daddy. I want to stay here. And I want Vera to stay here, too."

"You have a responsibility to your mother, you understand that?" He clenched his lips.

"I told you why we left Ransom, Frank," Vera whispered.

"Don't you think you overreacted a bit?" Daddy asked. "Jesus, just leaving without the courtesy of a good-bye."

"We left a note," Cissy said.

"Still . . ."

"*You* didn't say good-bye, either, Daddy. When you left. How come you left us? How come you left Ma?"

Cissy kicked him hard in the shin.

Daddy grabbed his leg and hopped around. "Ow! Why'd you go and do that?"

"I ain't going back there. I ain't! If anyone should, *you* should go back there and take care of Ma."

"Calm down." He rubbed his shin.

"Look at this." Vera lifted Cissy's shirt to show him the purply-black and yellow of the old bruise on her ribs. "Look at it, Frank. You don't know what it was like there."

Cissy pushed away Vera's hand, and pulled her

shirt back down over her bruises.

Daddy's face blanched. He turned away from them and stared out the window.

"Look at her arms," Vera said.

"Vera, no," Cissy pleaded.

"I don't need to see anything else." He was quiet. Thinking. Cissy could see the thoughts running around his head like little mice. Finally, he handed Vera the want ads. "I'll front you the first month's rent so you can get on your feet."

"Thank you."

"But, Daddy—"

"Look, kid, I'm sorry, I really am. But I can't have you here. I'm gone all the time, see?" He picked up his cup and walked down the hall. "Guess you got what you wanted, huh, Vera?"

"I never got what I wanted," Vera said. "I got what you and Rose wanted. You and Rose made all the decisions. Well, I'm making them now, Frank."

Daddy sighed. "I've got work to do," he said. "I'm taking a shower, so don't run the hot water."

"That's right, Frank, just run away from your problems like you always do."

"Shut up." He slammed the bathroom door shut.

"Welcome to the house of brotherly love," Vera muttered.

∞ ∞ ∞

Dear Beth,

Sorry I haven't written, but I am on the adventure to end all adventures! I am actually in Denver with my aunt Vera. We just decided, enough of Ransom, let's do something new. That Vera—she thinks of the craziest things. I saw my daddy, he looks just fine. I won't be staying with him, though, on account of his business. Besides, Aunt Vera needs me more, I think.

You wouldn't believe all the movie theaters here—I think I've died and gone over to the other side. I got a newspaper and I already circled the pictures I want to see, and me and Aunt Vera can go together. <u>China Seas</u> is playing here, so I'll send a full report later.

I can't write long, we're off to find an apartment, but know I miss you dreadfully.

Yours always,
Narcissus

Chapter Nineteen

"So the sink drips," Vera said. "It's as good as we're going to get for now."

Cissy's shoulders sagged. They had looked at ten apartments: None would take a lone woman with a thirteen-year-old girl in tow. Finally, ready to give up, they had called about an efficiency on Logan and Center. Yellow-gray paint peeled from the ceiling, the Murphy bed sagged, and the windows looked out on the smoky brick of another building. Still, the landlady, a tiny German woman with no more than three hairs on her head, had only lifted her hands, palms up, and said, "I stay out of people's business."

Vera and Cissy lugged Vera's sewing machine out of Frank's basement, and carried it the seven blocks from Frank's, then up the two flights to the apartment. Vera set to work making gingham curtains for the gaping cabinets. Cissy washed the coating of grease off the chipped cups, saucers, and plates that came stocked in the shabbily furnished apartment.

The sun dropped behind the next building, and the single overhead lamp shed a dull glow that didn't quite reach the four corners of the room.

Cissy turned on the light in the bathroom. "Well, at least we got hot and cold water."

Vera ran her arm over her forehead and sat back from the sewing machine. "I'm starving. Let's get something to eat. I know a good Chinese place close by."

"Chinese? I ain't—haven't—never had that."

"Well, throw on your dress, then, and we'll go."

It wasn't as dark outside as in. As much as Cissy breathed, she couldn't get the smell of exhaust out of her nose. Thunder rumbled far away, and every so often a flash of lightning brightened the dusky sky.

They took a trolley to South Pearl Street, then walked across the street to Chef Lee's. A light-blue neon sign flashed off and on, and red lights chased around the restaurant windows. Cissy didn't think she'd seen a more sophisticated sight, at least, not in real life.

They sat in a high-backed booth. "It's so fancy!" Cissy said.

Vera laughed out loud. "Wait'll I take you someplace really fancy."

The waiter approached.

"Bring me one of those little blue drinks. With the umbrella," Vera said. "A Coca-Cola for her. And we'll have the Family Special." She watched the waiter walk away, then continued. "Are you disappointed?"

"With what?"

"I know you wanted to live with your daddy, honey. I'm sorry."

A bitter taste lay on Cissy's tongue. "Guess he just don't want me."

"Oh, honey . . ."

Who did want her? Here she was, in a new city, in a new life, and still she stood on an island, adrift. "Sometimes I wish I was never born. Everyone would've been a lot happier."

"Don't ever say that. When you were born, it was the happiest day of my life. You just got stuck in a family that didn't work. But now you and I have a chance to make our own family. This time, we're going to make it work right."

"You promise?"

"I promise. And I never break my word."

Cissy looked at her aunt, at the sketch of worry warring with the bright optimism that was usually in her eyes. It startled her and sent a ripple of unease through her body.

A spattering of rain hit the plate glass window, sounding like the drumming of a hundred fingers.

"Oh, Vera, look!" Cissy jumped up, pushed open the heavy door of the restaurant, and spread her arms wide. The cold water slid down her cheeks and cooled her arms. She opened her mouth, letting the drops bounce on her tongue. A big timpani drumroll of thunder echoed against the buildings. A woman covered her head with her purse and ran for cover under an awning. Rain! Wet and wonderful and freezing. It amazed Cissy how cold the drops were, and how they sizzled on the cement.

She gestured for Vera to come outside, but Vera pointed to the food now sitting on the table. The rain gushed down, and Cissy jumped into the water streaming down the gutter. She wiggled her toes, hearing them squeak against each other in her shoes. Then as suddenly as the rain had started, it stopped. Cissy searched the skies for more.

Vera tapped against the window, motioning Cissy back inside.

Cissy pulled open the door, and people turned to look at her like she was out of her mind. Realizing what a fright she must look with her hair and dress plastered against her, she couldn't help but smile.

"Rain, Aunt Vera. Can you believe it?" Cissy laughed so hard her sides ached. "Makes everything clean and new and bright, don't it?"

Vera reached across the table and touched Cissy's cheek. "It'll be all right, honey."

"You got sauce on your blouse," Cissy said.

"What?" Vera looked down at the dark stain. "Well, look at that. The rain certainly won't clean that up."

Cissy laughed again. She laughed at Aunt Vera and she laughed for the rain and she laughed at the way the sky thundered with possibility.

The next morning, Vera flicked the paper in frustration. "Housekeeper . . . housekeeper . . . hosiery model . . . Servants! Look at this." Vera pointed to the Men's Help Wanted ads. "If I was a man, I could be a salesclerk, or work in a bank, or, I don't know what, get my old typing job back. New Deal, my foot—New Deal for men. You know, last year they took away my job at Gates Rubber Company and gave it to a man with three children. Said he had priority in these times, because he had more mouths to feed. As if it's just fine and dandy for a single woman to starve."

Cissy stepped from the bathroom, rubbing a washcloth over her face. "Why don't you go back and tell them you got a dependent, now? Tell them you took in an orphan."

"I will never cross that doorstep again."

"I could go to work, too, Aunt Vera. I saw that movie theater by Chef Lee's, and I could see if they need an usher. I have experience."

"No, honey, you're going to school."

"But we need money."

"September fourth. You will be in school on September fourth. How they all let you run around Ransom with nothing better to do than make dust pies and howl with the cats is beyond me." Vera buried her face in the want ads. "*I* will work, *you* will learn. One of us has got to get smart."

Cissy pulled a wobbly chair next to Vera and scanned the ads. "Look, we could buy a car. There's a used Nash cab for one hundred forty-five dollars. Wouldn't that be fine?"

"Look at the jobs, please."

"How about this one?" Cissy pointed near the bottom of the page. "'Woman between twenty-five and thirty-five for dining room and general work in cafe. Call Sunday.'"

"Hmmm. Maybe we'd get free food." Vera frowned, then grabbed a pencil, licked the tip, and circled the ad.

They heard heavy steps on the stairs. Daddy's voice boomed out, "Open the door, will you? This thing is heavy."

Vera pulled her robe closed, smoothed the covers on the Murphy bed, and opened the door. Frank dragged a fold-up cot into the room.

"Here. There's no need for you two to share one bed." Daddy opened the narrow cot and slid it between the wall and the Murphy. "Good, it fits." Running a handkerchief across his forehead, he made a quick scan of the room. "You've done nice things here. Hey, Cissy, try out the bed, see how it works."

"Okay." Cissy lay down on the narrow cot, and put her hands tightly against her sides. "It's swell, Daddy."

"It's been in the basement awhile. Leave it open to air out." He turned to Vera. "Still in your pajamas?"

"It's only eight o'clock, Frank. I hope you didn't wake up everyone in the building."

He flicked a piece of lint off his gray suit, then rubbed his hands together. "Cissy, I thought I might take you to Elitch's this morning. Get a little visit in before I have to take off again."

Cissy bolted up. "Elitch's? Really? Oh, boy, Jonas'll be so jealous. I'll go get dressed. I'll be ready in a minute. I can't wait to ride the roller coaster." She grabbed her dress and headed for the bathroom.

Elitch's Gardens exploded with color: red carnations, pink and fuchsia tulips, yellow marigolds, and green elms that gave cool shade and a place to rest.

Cissy watched the blooms shrink away as each *click clank clack* of the roller coaster took them higher and higher. The drop from the pinnacle felt the same as falling from consciousness, that momentary jerk between sleep and waking when the body loses all control. They flew by white crossbeams of wood, dipping and circling through a million sparking colors, up toward the blue sky, tossed toward the hard earth, then around again toward the heavens. She screamed with excitement. Daddy laughed and put an arm around her.

As suddenly as the ride began, it ended with a hard thump. Cissy stepped out of the cart, her body still filled with flight, and the cement beneath her moved and swayed.

"That was spectacular, Daddy. *Spectacular*."

They watched couples dancing near the big bandstand, played the ring toss, and through it all, Cissy melted into Daddy's strong comfort.

In the car on the way home, Cissy was sure Daddy would ask her to move in with him. They had gotten along fine today. Maybe he'd just been afraid that they would argue, like her and Ma.

Daddy put his open palm out the window against the breeze. "Listen, I'm headed for Wyoming for a few days. I'll call you when I get back in town."

Cissy's heart squeezed. They had had such a good time. "I wish you didn't have to leave."

"Look, I, uh . . . This is just the way it is, Cissy. I'm very busy. I'm lucky to be working."

"I wish things could be all right with you and Vera and we could live with you. We'd take care of the house and fix you dinner and—"

"It won't work, Cissy. Besides, you're going to have to go home eventually. Maybe you're being here for a bit will let you and your ma cool off. Give each other a break. Then when you go back, things'll be better."

"I ain't going back."

"You have a responsibility, Cissy. You might as well face it."

"I don't want to talk about it now. I got a new life now." She closed her eyes. She remembered the roller coaster, the pierce of blue as it climbed its way to the top. How the world sizzled as the cart fell. How, if she just raised her arms, she could fly.

"I'm sorry about Rose. I'm sorry she hurt you."

"I said I don't want to talk about her."

"Fair enough." He seemed relieved to drop it.

Chapter Twenty

Cissy recognized the woman leaning near the window in the apartment. The image was seared in her brain. The woman was swathed in white from her platinum-blond hair to the sheen of satin clinging along her body all the way down to the tips of her sequined shoes. Cissy couldn't take her eyes off her; she looked as though she'd just stepped out of a Tyrone Power picture.

"I'd like you to meet Maxine, honey," Vera said. "She's a friend of mine."

"Hello." Maxine laughed. "Well, well, well, well. This is a funny thing, isn't it?"

Cissy didn't quite know what was funny. Was Maxine laughing at her?

Maxine raised a penciled eyebrow at Vera. "She looks like her mother."

"No, I don't," Cissy said. "I look like my daddy."

Vera coughed and opened the icebox. "I didn't

expect you back for hours, Cissy. You thirsty? Here, sit down and have some milk." She sloshed the milk into a glass, set it on the table, and pointed at the chair. "Drink up."

"I'm not thirsty," Cissy said.

"Maxine sings at the Blue Parrot," Vera said. "That's the fancy place I was talking about. It's a jazz club. In fact, she's on her way there now, aren't you, Maxine?"

"You're talking a mile a minute," Cissy said.

"Am I?" Vera put a hand to her breast and sat down with a thud on the edge of the Murphy bed.

Maxine gave a little half smile and folded herself into the chair next to Cissy. "So, I hear you ran away from home."

Cissy shot a hard look at Aunt Vera.

"How was Elitch's, honey?" Vera asked.

"It was swell. Did you find a job?"

Vera stood, then sat right down again. "Shouldn't your taxi be here, Max?"

"Why don't you come to the show tonight?" Maxine asked.

"Tonight?" Vera's eyes widened.

Maxine kept her eyes on Cissy, but said to Vera, "I'd love to see you there."

"Not tonight," Vera said.

"Please, Aunt Vera?" Cissy wanted more than anything to hear Maxine sing. Going to the Blue Parrot would be like stepping onto the silvery screen. And it would be a chance to get out of the steaming apartment, with its close walls and loud neighbors.

"Some other time, then," Maxine purred. She turned at the sound of a horn blaring outside. "That's my cab." Maxine held her hand out to Cissy. "Welcome to Denver." Then she floated over to Vera, leaned down, and touched her cheek. "Sorry you'll miss the show." Maxine glided out the door.

"How was Elitch's?" Vera asked.

"You already asked me that."

"Oh." Vera ran a hand through her curls. "Are you hungry?"

"No. We ate. Why're you so nervous?" Cissy curled up beside her aunt.

"I'm not. Maxine came over unexpectedly, that's all." Vera blew out a long breath. "Actually, she brought me some sad news. About the loss of a mutual friend."

"Who's that?" Cissy asked.

"Um . . . let's see . . . Harry. You remember my letters about Harry, don't you, honey?"

"Sure. You sent a picture." Cissy lay back on the bed, resting her head on her hands. "Was Harry the reason you came to Ransom?"

Picking at a chip in the nail polish on her thumb, Vera said, "Not exactly."

Cissy sat straight up. Of course, she thought, it

made perfect sense. Vera had fallen for Harry without knowing he had a wife. He broke her heart and she ran away. "Was he married?"

"Who?" Vera asked. "Oh! Harry."

"Yeah, Harry. Were you in love with a married man?"

Vera smiled suddenly, then laughed until her shoulders shook. "I only wish it was that simple."

Chapter Twenty-one

"I don't need anybody to take care of me," Cissy said.

Maxine stood in a shaft of white morning sunshine. "I know that. But Vera's a little, you know, protective. She just wants what's best for you."

Cissy stuck her hands deep in the pockets of her dungarees. Vera hadn't been able to find any work for a week, and there wasn't much left of Mack's money, not after the bus fare and material for curtains, and the radio Vera "just *had* to buy."

"I've done perfectly fine all week while she's looked for jobs," Cissy said. "I'm thirteen years old. I'm almost old enough to be out on my own."

"You're absolutely right."

"Just so you understand that."

Maxine smiled. "I do."

"Okay, then."

Cissy didn't like the way Maxine sat down cross-legged on the bed like she owned it. She didn't like the way Maxine just stared at her with a funny half-lit smile. But she did like that she wore slacks. Just like Cissy.

"Why're you looking at me like that?" Cissy asked.

"Like what?"

"Like you know something you're not telling me."

Leaning back against the wall, Maxine said, "So, your father's out of town for a few days?"

"Maybe," Cissy said.

"I thought we could go to a picture show. *China Seas* is playing at the Mayan. My treat. I'd like to see what Clark's up to these days."

"You know him?"

Maxine shrugged. "I met him once or twice. I went out to Hollywood for a screen test. Ten years ago."

"You did?"

"He was a bit player, then. Probably much nicer than he is now."

"How come you ain't in the movies?"

"Ten years ago, there wasn't any sound in movies. Not much use for a singer in silent pictures," Maxine said with a laugh.

The telephone jangled downstairs in the hallway. Cissy listened for the holler of the landlady; after all, it might be Daddy. The phone rang steadily from eight A.M. to ten P.M. (no later, as the landlady took it off the hook for the night), but Cissy had yet to be called to it.

"Rossini!"

The lucky Rossini ran to the phone.

Cissy picked at the thick denim of her pants. "You're friends with my daddy, aren't you? I saw a picture of you all together."

"I liked him once. Not anymore."

"Why not?"

"It doesn't matter."

"It matters to me," Cissy said.

Maxine looked directly at Cissy. "You shouldn't put so much faith in that man."

Cissy stood up to get away from her stare. "Why don't you just leave?"

Maxine walked over to her and put a light hand on her shoulder. She smelled faintly of gardenias. "I'm sorry. I shouldn't have said that."

Cissy jerked away from Maxine. "Listen, I know how to take care of myself. And I don't need you hanging around."

"What if I just show you around the city?"

"Why don't you just pretend to, and I'll do it myself," Cissy said. "Vera doesn't need to know."

Smiling, Maxine said, "I like you, kid. You've got some guts." She stuck out her hand. "Deal."

∞ ∞ ∞

Dear Beth,

I hope you haven't sent any letters to the old house, which I fear you may have. I've been holding on to all of these letters to you, waiting for you to send an address. You didn't lose mine, did you?

Aunt Vera got a job! She's working as a waitress in a small diner on South Broadway. And you wouldn't believe the movies I've seen. These aren't just theaters, just images projected on a blank wall like down at Mack's. No, Beth, these are movie <u>palaces</u> with red-coated ushers and plush seats and screens as big as an acre of land! I've seen <u>Anne of Green Gables</u> twice, and <u>China Seas</u> and <u>Call of the Wild</u>—but my favorite so far has been <u>Naughty Marietta</u>— boy, can Jeannette MacDonald sing.

Which reminds me, I haven't told you about Maxine. She's a friend of Vera's, and if you weren't looking straight you'd swear she was Jean Harlow, slumming it in Denver. She sings at a club called the Blue Parrot. Vera says we're going there sometime, but she's squirrelly about when. In fact, she's squirrelly about Maxine. Too many secrets around here for me, and nobody answering any questions.

Maxine and I got this deal where we pretend to spend the days together (Vera still thinks of me as a <u>child</u>), but really I just make things up that Maxine and I did and pass it off as the truth. See, Beth, Maxine treats me like an <u>adult</u>.

I haven't seen my daddy in a while. I go by the house every day, but he isn't ever there. I swear to you, I know him best from his pictures and postcards. Salesman's life, huh?

Denver is certainly an exciting place. I've learned where all the trolleys go, and Beth, the things I've seen! There's a big country club here where ladies step out of long, shiny cars and do nothing all day but wear mink and eat lunch.

Down near the Platte River, all the trains crisscross and hook up to other trains and head off for Santa Fe, and Los Angeles, and Idaho, and I just don't know where else. All the tracks make me buzz, with their unknown destinations and stories.

And also down by the river is another world of shanties and screaming babies and skinny dogs. Yesterday, I picked my way through rusting cans and bed frames, walking down the winding rows of cardboard that were people's homes. I have to tell you, I feel sorry for these people. I mean, Vera and I got money problems, but it isn't nothing like this.

I turned a corner, Beth, trying to get out of there, covering my mouth against the stinky smell of cabbage, and thought I saw Ma. I about had a heart attack. This woman had the same red hair, and I tell you, I wanted to run as fast as I could to get away. But then this woman turned toward me, and she was too old to be Ma. She had the kindest, saddest eyes I've ever seen; it about cracked my heart wide open. And Beth, I went right up to her and gave her a hug. I think it made her feel better, too.

It's funny, Beth, how much I can miss my mother. I know she wasn't nice like yours, but she had some moments. I try to remember the old times—that's when I miss her most. But mostly, I miss little Fairbanks. He sure is a cute squiggly dog.

Anyway, enough of that. Wish you was here with me.

Yours always,
Narcissus

Chapter Twenty-two

In the apartment hallway, Cissy held her breath, staring at the telephone. Everything was so different in Denver; Cissy was beginning to feel lonely. She needed to hear a familiar voice.

She picked up the receiver, gave the operator the number, and waited.

"Hellooo?" Dotty's voice crackled through the wires.

"Dotty?" Cissy said.

"Yes? Who's this?"

"You know who it is. Cissy Funk. Could you go down the street and get Mack to pick up? I'll wait." The line popped, and for a minute, Cissy thought Dotty had hung up on her. "Dotty?"

"My word, we didn't know what had become of you. The whole congregation's been praying—"

"Please, Dotty, it's long distance. Go on over to the Odeon and put Mack on the phone."

"Why, he's up to Sterling today."

Cissy heard other breaths besides Dotty's. Damn party line. Everyone loved to listen in on everyone else's business.

"Cissy?"

Cissy closed her eyes and leaned her forehead against the wall. No. Not Ma. She felt dizzy.

Ma's even breath came over the line.

"Ma? Ma? You there?"

Breathing, only breathing.

"How are you? How's Fairbanks? Ma? Have you heard from Jonas?" Cissy wanted to beat her hand against the wall, to scream, to do anything to get Ma to talk, to get all the other busybodies off the phone.

The line crackled and hissed.

"I will never forgive you," Ma said.

"What?"

"You heard me. Never."

Cissy sank to the floor. She dropped the receiver, letting it bang against the wall and swing loosely on its cord. Then she hid her head in her arms and allowed the numbness to come. It could have been hours or minutes before she felt Vera's warm hand on her arm.

Cissy slowly looked up at her aunt. She held out her arms, stiff from being curled against the wall, and grabbed onto Vera.

"Cissy? What on earth happened?"

"Ma. Ma was on the line."

"You called her?"

"I didn't! I called Mack. She was just . . . there. And she wouldn't talk to me. Except to say she'd never forgive me. She hates me. For leaving her. I shouldn't have left her. I hate myself for leaving. I hate myself." Cissy lay her cheek on her aunt's shoulder and cried.

"You listen to me, Cissy Funk. You're strong and brave and you have the whole world before you. Don't you ever forget that. The way your ma is . . . it's not to do with you. Some of her hurt—well, the Lord gave Rose more than she had the strength to handle. But some of the hurt she brought on herself. She's not well, and that's not your fault." Vera pulled a hanky from her purse and wiped Cissy's cheeks. "Now, then, I'm thinking I've been working much too hard, and that you and I need to have some fun. So how about we do something wild and put this all behind us? Let's dress you up in one of my fanciest dresses and go hear Maxine sing at the Blue Parrot."

"We can't afford it."

"Of course we can, honey. We're friends of the star."

In the apartment, Vera fiddled with the knob on the radio, then swung open the closet door.

"We couldn't afford the radio, either."

"I cannot live without music, Cissy, you know

that. Now, be a good girl and try on this dress."

Cissy put on the dress Vera handed her. It was definitely Vera's style—mango silk with big purple flowers. The dress clasped at her neck, and scooped low on her back. It made her feel embarrassed and glamorous all at once. She knew she couldn't bend over in the dress, unless she wanted the world to see in the sides. And she most definitely did not want that. When Vera handed her a thin red sweater to put over the whole thing, Cissy breathed a sigh of relief.

She tried to shove Ma's words into the hollowness of her heart, but they hissed and burned. For Aunt Vera's sake, Cissy forced a smile. They were going to the club. They were going to pretend that Ma didn't exist and that they were not so very low on money.

Pretend to be someone else, Cissy thought. *Just pretend.*

Chapter Twenty-three

The club shimmered in twilight blue, as if the moon had been invited in for the evening. Satin draped the walls, the polished bar reflected the blue lights hung from above, the glossy black floor looked clear enough to swim in.

The Dirty Thirties, as so many people down on their luck called the times, didn't exist here. The epaulets on the hat girl's jacket shone, the men's top hats glowed, and not a wrinkle nor a missing button could be found in the diners' clothing. Big Ed Johnson, the governor himself, stopped by and shook hands, promising a brighter future and brand-new buildings. Hands held money, not dust, and people spoke of tomorrows with a smile.

Cissy sidled between two men in black tuxedos, the thin material of her borrowed dress sliding coolly against her leg. "I'll have a martini, please," she said. "Dry."

The bartender wiped a rag on the counter. "Oh, you will, will you?"

"A dry martini. Shaken to a waltz."

"And a Manhattan should be shaken to a fox-trot, and the Bronx to a two-step."

Cissy smiled. "You know it?"

He leaned his elbows on the bar. "Nick Charles, of course."

"*The Thin Man!* Didn't that picture just beat the band?"

"Never saw it."

"Then how'd you—"

"Do you have any idea how many people say that? Think they're some movie star, or something. 'Shaken to a waltz, shaken to a waltz' over and over again. Well, all we got is jazz." He emphasized his point with a big nod.

"Okay, then, shake it to jazz."

"I'll give you a cream soda, kid."

"It's not for me, it's for her." Cissy pointed to the table near the dance floor where Vera sat with Maxine.

"Then she can come up here and order it."

"I'm not going to drink it," Cissy said. "I'm just going to carry it."

"You want me to lose my job?"

"No."

"How'd you get in here, anyway?"

"I'm a friend of Maxine's." Saying it made Cissy feel important.

He chuckled. "A friend of Maxine's, huh? Well, all right, then." He handed her the soda in the inverted triangle of a martini glass. "Here's your cream soda. Dry."

Cissy walked back to the table and sat down.

"Don't slouch, honey, or button the sweater." Vera said. "I can see right in the side of that dress."

Cissy buttoned the red sweater all the way to the top. She had thought the dress the most beautiful thing in the world earlier; now, she felt afraid to move.

"Where's the martini?" Vera asked.

"He wouldn't give it to me."

"Oh, baloney," Maxine said. She pressed her lips together to even out her lipstick. "He only said that so you'd go talk to him, Vera. Go order two, Cissy, and tell him it's on my tab."

"I'll try." Cissy approached the bar again.

"Didn't I make myself clear? She has to come order it herself," the bartender said.

Vera waved from across the room, then clasped her hands together with a pleading look. Maxine rolled her eyes, gesturing for him to hurry up.

"Two, please. Put it on Maxine's tab," Cissy said.

"All right, all right. Dames."

Cissy took the glasses by the stems. "Thanks."

"What's your name, kid?"

"Cissy."

"Cissy? Just 'Cissy'?"

"Cissy Funk."

He glanced toward Vera, then stepped aside to take money from another customer. "She your mother?"

"Vera?" Cissy laughed. "No, she's my aunt."

"Well, Cissy Funk, you tell Vera that her old friend Tony would like to say hello." He straightened his black bow tie. "Now, go sit down; the show's about to start."

The band, wearing matching light blue jackets, tuned up. Maxine pinched Vera's cheek, then walked across the black marble dance floor and up to the microphone on the stage. The bandleader, in a tux with tails, smiled and waved as he came out from behind a gossamer curtain. He nodded to Maxine, then turned to the band. Everybody hushed, leaning forward in their seats. The only sound was the clink of glassware at the bar.

The strings came first, followed by the jolt of horns. Maxine opened her mouth, and her voice came out meltingly warm, like a long summer sunset. The stage lights glistened along the sequined curve of her hip, and sent sparkles from her rhinestone necklace. She winked at Cissy.

The wash of music and black coats and fur stoles and blue satin walls made Cissy feel the way she had felt on the roller coaster. Like she really could fly. Like everything was all right and Cissy could be anyone she wanted. Anyone but herself.

Arm in arm, Cissy, Vera, and Maxine sang at the top of their lungs one of Maxine's songs.

They climbed up the stairs to the apartment, and Vera clicked on the light. "Oh, it's hot in here."

The heat wrapped around Cissy. She was more tired than she'd ever been. But alive. So absolutely alive. The light spun around in circles, even when she lay on her narrow bed and closed her eyes.

"You all right?" Maxine asked.

"Just tired." Cissy yawned and stretched out her arms. "I'm gonna go to sleep now." She went in the bathroom to change into her pajamas, then crawled onto the cot. The images of the evening flickered across her eyelids, the edges gilded with the beginning of sleep.

"I want to stay the night," Maxine whispered to Vera.

"You need to go home," Vera said. A bottle clinked on the table. "Graham'll wonder where you are."

"He won't even notice." She paused. "I think I should just move in here with you."

"What?" Vera said.

"We like each other a whole lot more than we like anyone else. It'd be fun."

"You're nuts."

"Frank'll have a nice little heart attack and disappear from our lives."

"I promised Frank I wouldn't see you. But I can't help it, can I?" There was a small moment of quiet, then Vera said, "Cissy?"

Cissy shut her eyes tighter and pretended to sleep.

Vera lowered her voice. "You need to go home, Max."

"Let me stay."

Something clear and bright flashed at the side of Cissy's mind. It was an answer without a question, and the more she grasped for it, the quicker it slid away. She dropped down a long tunnel, jerked once, then let her body reach the fuzziness of sleep.

It was a dance on a deep blue floor. It was Vera twirling Cissy. It was laughter spun like music, like jazz. It was mango sky and pink trees and purple roses. Maxine floated by on a cloud of her own voice. A man with a trombone took a seat and played. Vera let go of Cissy, leaving her in a circle of red. A calico cat stood on its head and hissed.

153

Cissy screamed without sound. She was trapped on her isle of red with a cat whose claws gleamed white. Vera and Maxine danced on, oblivious. The trombone man quit playing.

And the cat smiled wide.

Chapter Twenty-four

"Ooh . . ." Maxine groaned and sat up in bed. "I'm getting too old to stay up so late. My head."

Cissy peeked out from under her pillow. Maxine wore no makeup, and in the morning sun her eyelashes were almost as blond as her hair.

Vera walked back from the kitchen and handed Maxine a wet towel. She then sat in a chair, tilted her head back and covered her own face with another cold rag. She blew out a muffled sigh. "I have got to get ready for work." Then she stood and walked over to Cissy's bed. She pulled the cover over Cissy's shoulder and lightly touched her hair. "She's something, isn't she?"

Cissy snored a little, just enough so it didn't seem forced.

"She's a good kid." Maxine lowered her voice. "And you should tell her."

"I tell her all the time."

"You know what I mean."

"I've ruined her life once. I'm not going to do it again," Vera whispered.

"So much easier to be a savior."

"*Enough*, Max." Vera reached over and shook Cissy's shoulder. "Honey? Rise and shine. Time to meet the day."

"It's morning already?" Cissy asked.

"Why don't you run down to the corner and get some milk and a copy of the *Post* from the grocery? I'd do it, but I'm late as it is."

"I'd do it," Maxine said, "but the dead don't move."

Cissy pulled on her dungarees over her pajamas and took some change from the cash jar on the counter. Over her shoulder, she said to Maxine, "Hope your husband doesn't mind you're here."

"Don't talk about my husband so early, please."

"Cissy!"

"I'm going," Cissy said. "I'm going."

She touched the receiver on the hallway phone, placing a wish for a call from Daddy, and remembering the sting of Ma's words. She'd never make the mistake of calling again. Outside, the sky choked with ochers and browns, signal of a faraway dust storm. She'd read of a Minnesota couple who woke up to find their deep black soil brilliant red with the clay of Oklahoma. Cissy wiped her eyes. Dull and nut-brown, this was Colorado dirt for sure.

Mr. Jacobs stood behind the cash register, tapping his pocket watch on the glass counter. His big, walrus mustache wriggled up into a W when he caught sight of Cissy. "Look at this." He held the watch up by its chain. "Piece of dirt in the wheels. That's the second one this year."

"I've seen worse," Cissy said. She set her money on the counter.

"Sad news today."

The *Denver Post* headline blazed out in bold, black letters.

WILL ROGERS AND WILEY POST DIE WHEN PLANE CRASHES IN ALASKA.

"No!" Cissy said.

Bodies Found in Wreck After Dive in River. Both Men Killed Thursday in 50-ft. Fall.

Cissy licked a salty tear from the corner of her mouth. "Don't know why I'm crying." She wished life was more like the movies; movies ended and no one good died. Endings could always be counted on. Not like real life, where someone you didn't know, but also loved deeply, could just disappear, leaving only ink on a news page for solace.

So she cried for the man who never met anyone he didn't like.

Cissy sprawled on the Murphy bed and spread the paper before her. She turned the pages, past testimonials to Will Rogers, and ads for Woolworth's and J. C. Penney.

"Hey, Maxine?"

"Hey, what?" Maxine answered.

"You sing as good as Billie Holiday. You could be on the radio. I bet you could even go back to Hollywood, now that there's sound, and I bet you'd get a seven-picture contract."

Maxine laughed. "You think so?"

"I know so." Cissy went back to the newspaper, turned a page, and said very, very casually, "I was wondering something, Maxine. How did Aunt Vera ruin my life?"

Maxine sucked in her breath. "Little pitchers have big ears."

"I'm not so little. Anyway, I just happened to overhear."

"Talk to Vera." Maxine lay back on the bed and covered her face with a pillow.

Well, so much for that. Cissy wondered how Vera could have ruined her life. How? And how come no one ever told her the real, live facts? She shook her head. As she turned another page, her heart saw the bold ad almost before her eyes did.

"Oh, my gosh, I don't believe it! This is spectacular! Maxine, look!"

Maxine slid on a pair of round wireframe glasses and studied the ad. "One dollar?"

"But they fly you to Hollywood," Cissy said. "You get a screen test. Maybe I'd meet Judy Garland or Myrna Loy or, I don't know who! We gotta go to the cafe to show Aunt Vera."

159

"I've never heard of Pinnacle Pictures."

"Oh, Maxine, I've got to do it. Don't you see? It's what I've wanted all my life." Cissy felt ready to burst.

"I don't know—"

"I could do it, I could win that. And it's September first. That's my birthday. That makes it even more lucky. Aunt Vera'll let me do it, I know she will."

Sliding her glasses down the bridge of her nose, Maxine looked at Cissy. "I believe Vera wants you to go to school, not to Hollywood."

Cissy sneered. "School? Who needs school when you can be in the pictures?" She jumped up and ran to the mirror in the bathroom. She tugged at her hair. "Why'd Vera make me cut this? I look like I'm ten."

"I'm not so sure about this."

"You can help me—you've been to Hollywood."

Maxine laughed. "Well, if you're going to be a star, you'll have to learn how to walk and enunciate, and . . . we'll have to curl your hair . . . a little makeup so you don't look like a ghost, and—"

Cissy grabbed onto Maxine and hugged. "I knew you'd help me. And if I win, we'll all move to California."

Maxine laughed again, then winced and grabbed her head. "How will I make it through rehearsal?"

∞ ∞ ∞

160

Dear Beth,

Maxine LaTrelle will be a name to remember. She's the best singer I've ever heard, and I'll bet she gets a radio show one of these days. I'll also wager she's as good as anything you can hear out in sunny Los Angeles.

And now THE BIG NEWS: I am auditioning for a movie company!!! Maxine (who's been to Hollywood) is going to help me get ready. She says I still have to work on saying "aren't" instead of "ain't" and other such "country bumpkin" words. And I'm going to learn to walk like a lady and wear makeup, and I'm even going to learn a whole speech.

Then I can win the contest and come visit you! Won't that just take the cake???

Yours always,
Louise LaFontaine
(My new screen name)

Chapter Twenty-five

Cissy loved Tuesday afternoons more than anything. Vera worked only breakfasts on Tuesday, and she'd meet Cissy in Washington Park, holding a bag of jelly donuts they'd share with each other and the ducks in the pond.

Sitting on a park bench, waiting for Vera, Cissy watched a young girl with Shirley Temple curls play hopscotch across the street. The house behind the girl had beveled windows, and the sunlight played on the cut glass, sending sparks of rainbows across the perfectly mowed grass. A great elm tree shaded the girl playing hopscotch. The shade looked greener and cooler on her side of the street. Cissy counted the windows. Five windows on the second floor alone. Only four on the first floor, but they ran floor to ceiling. Cissy thought the house far too big for this solitary and very little girl.

Behind the house, in the distance, the Rocky

Mountains lay blue and gray. To the west, Mount Evans shimmered in and out of view. Cissy wanted to go to the top of the mountain, to see if it shimmered as beautifully when you were right up close.

Cissy heard Vera call her name. Vera picked her way across the grass waving a white envelope in one hand. In the other, she held the dreamed-of-all-week greasy bag of donuts and pie.

She sat down, dropped the bag on the bench next to her, and then wrapped her arm around Cissy and squeezed tight. She kissed her twice on the head. "You smell so sweet."

"So do you—like grape-jelly donuts."

"Those old grape things are for the ducks," Vera said. "Today, madam, I brought you a piece of lemon meringue pie, which, it must be stated, is the best pie in Colorado, if not the entire United States."

"What's the letter?"

Vera smiled, then blew a curl out of her eyes. "It's from the school, honey. I thought we might read it together and see what your institute of higher learning has to say."

While Cissy ate her piece of pie, using a piece of the brown bag as a plate, Vera opened the letter as if it came from the King of England himself.

"'This is to confirm that Narcissus Louise Funk will be attending the ninth grade at South High School.'—The ninth grade, honey. I'm so proud of you.—'Your child will need the following items,

and should bring them on the first day of school:
"'A dozen pencils
Five bound composition notebooks
Two erasers
A dictionary
Gym suit
Athletic shoes.'"

Vera looked the letter over. "Hmmm. That's a lot." She frowned, then folded the letter and stuffed it into her purse. "I'll have to ask for some dinner shifts. And you'll have to cut back on the movies."

Cissy held out the other half of her pie to her aunt. "Want some?"

"That's all right. I see pie all day long." She gazed across the pond. "And now I see Frank. Just what I need."

"Daddy!" Cissy ran around the edge of the pond, setting a group of geese running and diving into the water.

"Well, hey, kiddo."

"Whatcha doing?"

"Taking a breather between clients. What're you doing?"

"Scaring the geese," she said.

Daddy approached Vera and nodded. "I thought you had a job."

"I do have a job," Vera said. "This is my half day."

"Half days don't feed children."

"Don't start, Frank."

"I got my letter from school," Cissy said. "Want to see?"

"Why don't you give me the gist of it." Frank gave Cissy a thin smile.

"Well, hey, you got a bit of time, I got a bit of time—how about I come over?" Cissy asked. "I have so much news, you wouldn't believe it."

"No, Cissy. Let's go home, now." Vera stood up, hooking her purse over her arm.

"Can't I please, Aunt Vera?"

"Sure," Daddy said, "let's catch up."

"Playing at father, Frank?" Vera said.

"Playing at mother, Vera?" Daddy shot back.

Vera flinched. Then she stepped away from Cissy and Daddy. "Don't be late for dinner, honey."

Chapter Twenty-six

". . . and you get to go to Hollywood. I bet I'd see a million stars," Cissy said.

"Hand me those shears." Daddy pulled out a branch on a rosebush, careful to avoid the thorns, and snipped.

Cissy put her hands under her legs and leaned forward on the wooden folding chair in the yard. "What do you think? Think I could win?"

"What do you have to do?" Daddy asked.

"What do you mean?"

"Sing a song, dance, I don't know, something like that."

Cissy touched the silky petals. "Well, Maxine says I have to learn to walk like a lady and fix up my—"

"Maxine?"

"Oh, no." Cissy covered her mouth with her hand.

"Well, how is Maxine?"

"Um, I only met her once, Aunt Vera and I ran into her on a street corner. I barely remember what she looks like."

"Uh-huh."

"I mean, Aunt Vera promised you she wouldn't see Maxine, didn't she?"

"On a street corner, huh?"

"Yeah, um, Broadway and Mississippi, just one day out of the blue." If Daddy'd only stop staring at her. If only she could get him to think of something else. "Anyhow, the contest's on my birthday, so you could come over for cake and then watch me in the contest."

"That's September first, right? I wish I could come, darlin', but I'll be in Colorado Springs."

"You can't change your plans?"

"Afraid not. I'm sure you'll have a fun time with Vera. She may be a lot of things, but she's always fun."

"Yeah." Cissy wiped at her eyes.

"Aw, you're not going to cry, are you? I'm sorry I can't be at your party, but work's work."

"I'm not gonna cry." Cissy pinched the bridge of her nose. No, she wouldn't cry, wouldn't show him how much his answer hurt.

The telephone clattered inside, and Daddy went in to answer. Cissy followed.

"Frank Funk here. Well, hello . . ." Oh, how

167

Daddy's voice oozed smiles. He leaned against the wall and checked his hair in the mirror. "Me, too. Yeah . . . no, there isn't anyone here. Eight o'clock? Then eight it is. I'll be looking forward to it." He hung up and whistled a little. "You tell Vera I want to speak with her."

"Who was that?" Cissy asked.

"Never you mind."

"How come you told 'Never You Mind' there wasn't anybody else here?"

"How come you listen in on conversations that aren't your business? No wonder you drove your ma crazy."

Cissy looked at him. Really looked at him, past the memories she'd masked his face with. She saw a meanness she hadn't noticed before, and a blackness in his eyes that was unreadable and cold. There was no softness there when he looked at her, a softness she'd gotten from Aunt Vera. She'd even seen it in Maxine's eyes, a look that always made Cissy feel wanted. It wasn't in her father's eyes.

"Head on home, kiddo. And tell Vera I mean it. I need to talk to her. It's important."

Cissy nodded. There wasn't much else to do. She had been dismissed. "Yes, sir."

Dear Beth,
    I've spent the last two weeks walking with a book on my head, said "how now

brown cow" so many times I can't even look at a glass of milk, and practiced my speech, "Ode to a Grecian Urn," until I'm hoarse. I am almost ready, Beth!

Something mysterious is going on here. Remember I told you that Vera had a dreadful secret? Well, I think it's something to do with Maxine. Daddy was really funny asking about her the other day. I pretended I hardly even knew who Maxine was, because she's my friend and I wouldn't want anyone angry with her. When I told Aunt Vera that Daddy wanted to see her, that it was important, she turned all green and looked like she was going to be sick. And now Daddy keeps calling and calling, but he talks to Aunt Vera and not me, except to say hello.

The weird thing is that, sometimes, when they think I'm not watching, Aunt Vera and Maxine give each other funny kind of looks. And Maxine stays over at the house a lot. She's got a husband and everything, but I haven't ever met him, and she doesn't seem to like him too much.

I know Maxine is Vera's best friend in the whole world (just like you are to me, Beth), and she's been so helpful getting me ready for the contest, but still . . . it's very curious. She says she wants us all to move to a big house together without Graham (that's her invisible husband). But Aunt Vera pooh-poohs that idea any time Maxine brings it up and looks at me strangely, like the whole reason we all can't live together is because of me. I think it'd be fun, though.

Adults are screwy, aren't they? Let's stay kids forever!

Yours always,
Miss LaFontaine

P.S. This is my first birthday without you. Eat some cake and think of me.

Chapter Twenty-seven

The day before the contest, Maxine applied a line of kohl under Cissy's eye, then checked Cissy's face in the mirror. "There, see? That makes your eyes stand out."

Cissy turned up her lip. "Makes me look like a ghoul."

"The camera sees things differently."

Cissy bared her teeth like Dracula. "I vant to suck your blood."

"Hold still; it's not dry."

"Were you in Hollywood a long time?"

Maxine blew blush off a brush, then wiped Cissy's cheeks. "Long enough."

"Did you meet Theda Bara, or Mary Pickford?"

"I went to Pickfair once for a party."

"Is Douglas Fairbanks as handsome in real life?"

"More so," Maxine said. "Vera's late."

Cissy held up a lipstick. "Give me the 'It' look."

"That went out of fashion quite a while ago."

"Please? For fun?"

Cissy held very still, letting Maxine draw on tiny bow lips. She watched Maxine's nostrils flare in concentration, and her pale eyelashes flicker up and down.

"Did Vera ask you for any money?" Cissy asked.

"No. Why?"

"Just wondering. I think we're out."

Maxine pretended to be a big director. In her very best Eric von Stroheim accent, she barked, "Turn your head RIGHT. Turn your head LEFT. Ahhh, you are the most beautiful girl I've ever seen. After Garbo, of course." She touched Cissy's cheek and said, "You're ready."

Vera entered the room, closing the door quietly behind her. She set her purse on the kitchen table, then poured a glass of water from the tap.

"Aunt Vera, look! I'm Clara Bow, come back to haunt you."

Vera sat at the table, folding her hands in front of her. She watched Cissy with clouded eyes.

Cissy bounced on the bed and crossed her legs. "Are we having cake for my birthday tomorrow? I think we should have our party first, then go on down to the theater. So I can fully concentrate on the audition, you know."

Vera kept looking at Cissy or, rather, through her.

Maxine leaned against the kitchen counter. "Stayed late at work?"

"No."

"Then you must have been birthday shopping for someone we know." She winked at Cissy.

"It's been a very long day," Vera said.

"Well, sit on down, Aunt Vera, and I'll recite my speech for you. 'Ode to a Grecian Urn.'"

"Go wash your face, Cissy," Vera snapped.

"What's wrong, Aunt Vera?"

"I said go wash your face." Vera stood up. "Go home, Maxine."

"Excuse me?"

"I need to *think*. There's no room to think here." She whirled around. "Where's my hat?"

"On your head," Maxine said.

"I'm going for a walk."

"But you just got here," Cissy said.

"I can go out again if I want. It's a free country. When I get back, I want your face clean, Cissy." She glared at Maxine. "And I want you gone." Her hand trembled as she picked up her purse and walked out.

Cissy's chest tightened. Something was wrong. She could feel it like electricity, crackling and burning her veins. "Maxine?"

Maxine lifted her shoulders and gave Cissy a puzzled smile.

Chapter Twenty-eight

Turning in her bed, Cissy yanked the sheet to the floor and twisted her hip to avoid a hard spring in the thin mattress. The night air was so still and thick, she thought she could reach out a hand and grab a piece of it. She squeezed her eyes shut. She had to sleep, to be ready for the greatest day in her life, but the blackness evaded her.

Vera's bed remained empty. Cissy blew through her lips in frustration. This was not a night for strangeness, and her aunt was acting strange.

Cissy sat up with a start. It suddenly made sense. They had no money for rent. Maxine hadn't given Vera anything. Maybe Vera had lost her job and was afraid to tell Cissy.

She had to win the screen test. There was no choice. Oh, what time was it? Where was Vera? Cissy wanted to tell her everything would be all right; she'd take care of it. When would the night end?

The next time she opened her eyes, gray light filtered through the window. The sheet she had thrown off in the night now covered her. Vera sat at the table, still dressed from yesterday, her head in her hands, as if she had been too tired to hold it up any longer.

"Aunt Vera?"

Vera raised her head. Her eyes were puffy and red, ringed with dark circles. "Hmmm?"

"What time is it?"

Vera lifted the corner of her mouth in a heavy smile. "It's early, honey. Go back to sleep."

"I can't."

"You should try."

"I'm too excited," Cissy said. "I'm going to win today, I just know it."

"I'm not any good at this."

"At what?" Cissy asked. "You're not making any sense, Aunt Vera."

"You're right. I'm not." Vera stood and looked out the window. Cissy noticed how Vera's dress hung loose on her. Had she lost weight? Why hadn't Cissy paid more attention? She'd been so caught up with herself and the dumb contest. Something weighed heavily on Vera—something was terribly wrong.

"Aunt Vera, tell me. Is it your job? Are we having money problems? What's wrong?"

"Everything I try to do right always turns out

wrong." A tear glistened on Vera's cheek. She wiped at it roughly, then pointed a shaky finger at a thick, sealed envelope. "Here. I want you to pin this to your dress with your other pictures. And promise me you won't read it until tonight."

Cissy took the envelope and turned it over in her hands. "Is it my birthday card? Why can't I read it now?"

"I'm going to make your cake. You have to have a cake."

"With extra frosting?" Cissy asked.

"With extra frosting."

The tick of the clock on the stove and the clink of measuring spoons were the only sounds in the room. Cissy got dressed and pinned on the mysterious envelope. The dread she felt yesterday when Vera left now pervaded the room like a heavy, sickly sweet perfume.

Cissy thought she should scream, just to stir the air and shock Vera out of her silence. Thank God for Maxine. Thank God she showed up one second before Cissy was about to shake Vera by the shoulders.

"It smells like chocolate cake," Maxine said. "My favorite. Vera, you look terrible."

"Thank you so much."

Maxine set a small wrapped package on the table, then turned to Cissy. "Let's get your makeup on. Sit down in the chair."

Vera looked at her watch then at the door. "After you do that, I want to spend some time with Cissy. Alone."

"But Maxine's my birthday guest." Cissy closed her eyes as Maxine applied the powders and paints.

"Recite the poem," Maxine said.

"I know it. I feel if I say it now, I'll jinx it."

"Go like this with your mouth." Maxine stretched her lips over her teeth and Cissy followed suit. "Don't move." She licked the bristles of a tiny brush, rubbed it against a pot of red, and lined Cissy's lips. "When you get to Hollywood, Cissy, you remember me, all right? Don't act like a big shot."

"Sure. I'll send you an autograph. Do I look okay, Aunt Vera? Do I look like a star?" Cissy did her best Jean Harlow imitation, leaning back in the chair and looking through what she hoped were hooded lids.

Vera shook her head. "It's fine."

Maxine put her hands in the pockets of her trousers and glared at Vera. "What is wrong with you?"

Vera slammed the spatula down on the counter, sending specks of chocolate frosting flying onto the wall and floor. She passed the back of her hand over her forehead, picked up the spatula, and dug back in the frosting.

"Aunt Vera," Cissy said, "this is a very important

day to me, and I don't want it ruined."

"You're right. I'm sorry."

"Good," Maxine said. "Why don't we just start over?" Maxine frowned, then searched the room for something. "Vera, where's that old photo album of yours? There's such a cute picture in there of Cissy, I wanted to show her." She looked at Cissy. "I think you were, what, six? Five? Maybe you've already seen it, though." Maxine opened the album and smoothed the first page. "That's Vera when she was very, very little. You look a lot like her, don't you?"

"What are you doing, Maxine?" Vera said.

"I'm showing her the pictures. And, look, Frank had long droopy curls and short pants. Like Little Lord Fauntleroy, and just as spoiled." She turned the page.

Cissy pointed at a picture of Vera with her arms held straight at her sides and a big frown on her face. "How old are you there, Aunt Vera?"

"Oh, I must have been about your age."

"No one ever smiles in your pictures."

"It was the style of the time. The olden days." Maxine pulled the picture from its corners and held it next to Vera's somber face. "Some things never change."

"Give me that picture," Vera said.

"Why?"

"Because this isn't your business, Maxine.

Don't play around anymore."

Cissy's heart thudded. "Let me see that." She walked into the bathroom and held the picture of Vera next to her own face. Except for the hair color, Vera's black as ink next to Cissy's nut-brown, they could have been sisters. She'd never noticed the similarity before, the way their noses turned up just slightly and their eyes were rounded so exactly alike.

Vera walked up behind her, and Cissy caught her eyes in the mirror.

"Jonas and Violet had Ma's red hair. How come I don't?"

Vera took the photo out of Cissy's hands. "Sometimes children don't look anything like their parents. You wouldn't even know they're related."

"I don't care if I look like her anyway. She's ugly."

"Rose isn't ugly. Every man in Ransom had a thing for her at one time or another."

"She's ugly to me," Cissy said. "Witch's hair, that's what she's got. You look more like me than my mother does."

Vera's face paled. "That's silly. I look like your aunt."

Cissy said quietly, "I wish you were my mother." Her heart reached out when she said it.

Vera looked down, nodded once, then went

back to the kitchen table. "If wishes were horses, beggars would ride."

That's right, Cissy thought, and if all her wishes came true, she'd have a thousand horses. But this one—if only Vera had said she wished it, too.

"Don't you ever do that again, Maxine," Vera said.

Cissy peeked around the bathroom door. Aunt Vera's back was to her. Maxine leaned toward Vera and said, "Every day that goes by makes it worse." She noticed Cissy. "How about opening your present?"

Cissy picked it up. "It's a book." She ripped off the flowery paper and read the title. "*National Velvet*. Thanks, Maxine!"

"You're welcome. Thought you'd need some reading for the aeroplane ride to California. Give her your present, Vera."

Vera opened the closet and reached into a corner, pulling out a box. "I didn't have time to wrap it. I . . . here, honey."

Cissy opened the box and held up the shiniest, prettiest pair of Mary Janes she'd ever seen. Even the buckles glistened.

"I hope you like them," Vera said.

"Like them? I love them." Cissy slid the shoes on. "Perfect. They're perfect, Vera." She gave Vera a hug. "I love them."

"All right, the presents are done," Vera said. "So, Maxine, could you—"

A sharp knock came at the door.

Vera stiffened, then stepped away from Cissy and walked over to the window. The door snapped open, and Daddy came into the room.

"Daddy! I thought you were in Colorado Springs." He had come! He wasn't as mean as she'd thought him the last time. No, of course, he had only acted that way to cover this wonderful surprise.

"It's a good thing I didn't go, isn't it? What's that on your face? You look like a clown."

Cissy flailed her arms, trying to think of something to say. "I can't believe you came. This is the greatest present, isn't it, Aunt Vera?"

Vera turned away.

"You didn't tell her, did you," Daddy said.

"What are you doing here?" Maxine asked.

Daddy brushed Maxine aside and strode over to Vera. "Even today you couldn't have kept her away. Jesus, Vera. Well, is she ready?"

"Yes."

"Ready for what, Daddy?"

"Go wash that off your face, Cissy, and we'll be leaving."

"I don't understand," Cissy said.

"I'm taking you home to Ransom."

"No, you're not," Maxine said. "This is her home."

"And how's Vera going to afford to keep her without a job?" he asked.

The air drained out of the room. A moment passed; no one spoke or moved, but all eyes were on Vera.

"You lost your job?" Maxine asked.

Vera nodded.

"That's not a reason to send her back."

"Shut up, Maxine," Daddy said. "This has nothing to do with you."

Maxine spun on Daddy. "This has everything to do with me. Oh, I get it—you don't want Cissy around me, do you?"

"I want Cissy to go back to Ransom to take care of her family—because that's what a real family does."

"And Vera and I are a sham. Right, Frank?" The muscles in Maxine's jaws quivered with rage. "What the hell did you do, Vera?"

"There's no money," Vera whispered.

Cissy twisted away as Daddy tried to take her arm. "Aunt Vera, please! I don't want to go back. It's the contest—I can't miss the contest."

"Listen to your father, Cissy."

"I'm not going anywhere!" Cissy said. "I've got to go to the contest!"

"Don't make this harder than it is," Vera said. "Go with your father. I've packed your bag."

Cissy ran into the bathroom, slamming the

door. She turned on the faucet and looked in the mirror. As her tears began to fall, her eyeliner ran. She splashed water on her face and rubbed at the rouge, but the more she rubbed, the more the makeup smeared. Her face now looked like the face of a grotesque clown, no longer like that of beautiful glamour queen.

Unscrewing the cap from one of Vera's lipsticks, Cissy wrote "I HATE YOU" in red across the mirror.

"Let's go, Cissy," Daddy said through the door.

A calm settled over Cissy, deadly and silent and void. She held up her head and walked into the kitchen, feeling no emotion but emptiness.

Vera held her arms tightly across her chest. She rocked with grief. *Good*, Cissy thought. *Let her.*

"I wanted time to explain, honey. Frank, give me time to explain."

"I am a busy man, Vera. Come on, Cissy." He propelled her forward.

"But the contest, Aunt Vera. I could have won it. I could have made everything all right."

Vera never took her eyes off the floor.

Chapter Twenty-nine

Cissy stared out the car window as Daddy drove them past the Mayan Theater. The gold-and-red Pinnacle Pictures banner snapped against the brick building. With each eager face—there a girl in curls, there a man in a tux, there a baton thrower—Cissy felt her heart drop. She wished at that moment it would stop beating. Why not? There was no difference to her between physical death and the death of her dream. She could have been in the line just like everyone else, with a number pinned to her back and hope pinned to her heart.

Instead, she felt only numbness at Aunt Vera's betrayal. Jonas had been right. Everything was broken promises and secrets and lies. She couldn't trust anyone—not for love or anything else.

As they drove silently away from the city, Cissy became as hard as the brick buildings and paved streets. This time, she retreated to her island for solace. She was all she could count on. Inside, her heart lay in pieces, each bit angry and numb and full of tears.

The trolleys, the cement, the movie palaces, the cool satin of the Blue Parrot nightclub faded into beige earth, dried yellow grass, and olive-drab skies. At the edge of a sugar beet field, the paved road finally gave way to dirt, rutted and grooved. A dented truck poked down the road, a sofa tied onto the back of the truck, a sleeping child on the sofa. Little whirligigs of dust danced across the barren land, like demons relishing their power over the world.

The more open the plains became, the more hedged in Cissy felt. It was as if a wall was being built around her, a brick added with each mile. No matter where Cissy looked, Ma's house loomed before her like a drifting ghost, waiting to invite her in. She'd never get out again. The thought of seeing Fairbanks was her only comfort.

Frank cut the silence. "When I telephoned Rose, she was sure happy to hear you're coming home. She needs you, you know. Glad you came to your senses."

Cissy crossed her arms. "You tell me what other choice I got."

They sat in silence.

The streets of Ransom lay empty, minus a few rusty pickup trucks parked on Main Street and the three farmers lined up in their usual positions

185

against Jake's Bar. The wooden sign for the Hasty Twins butcher shop hung on one rung, slapping against the building.

"There's no life here," Cissy murmured.

They passed the Odeon and Blue Willow Cafe. No sign of Mack or Rusty or Lucille. Cissy half hoped Jonas would be sitting in front of the old Coronado Hotel, but he was hundreds of miles away.

The car crunched to a stop in front of the house. Frank wiped the sweat from his brow and stepped out of the car.

Cissy shrank into the corner of the seat. "I'm not going in."

"Get out of the car right now," Daddy said.

"No."

He leaned in toward her and smiled. "Look, kiddo, let's be reasonable here."

"No!"

"I swear to you, you will get your—"

She wouldn't go. She screwed up her hands, shoving them under her legs. Come hell or high water, she was not leaving the car.

Shaking his head, Daddy went inside the house.

A mound of dirt hugged the house's foundation and rolled over the bottom wire of the fence. Sheets, faded and gray, hung on the clothesline. The front windows looked as if someone had painted a fine veneer of dust on them, and as much as Cissy peered, she saw nothing but darkness inside. That's all this house ever was, had ever been—darkness.

A rusty, beat-up motorcycle roared up beside the car.

"Jonas!" Cissy pulled at the door handle, and fell out of the car, sending a cloud of grasshoppers fluttering around her. Wrapping her arms around him, she grabbed onto her brother's rough shirt.

"Hey, little sis. Missed you." His yellow-green eyes crinkled into a smile.

Then, Cissy felt Fairbanks's wet lick on her ankle, and she thought she might just crumble with happiness. She knelt down on the earth, and Fairbanks wriggled into her lap, licking her arm. "You remember me. You remember!"

"Want to take a ride?" Jonas asked.

"What about them?" Cissy looked to the house.

"They'll wait."

"Think you can get this machine out of the yard without a wheel falling off?" Cissy asked.

"Very funny." He swung his leg up and over the seat, then patted behind him. "Hop on."

The engine shook and vibrated. Cissy hung on to Jonas to keep from flying off the bike as it bounced over the ruts by the barn and behind the outhouse.

Gravel flew out from under the wheels as he steered the motorcycle onto the road, and Fairbanks, who had followed in the yard, finally gave up and loped back to the house. As Jonas made a sharp turn by the cemetery, the bike hiccuped and popped, then died.

"Ah, hell," Jonas said.

Cissy got off the motorcycle, then watched Jonas fiddle with it. She wiped her Mary Janes against the backs of her bare legs. The buzz of grasshoppers made the dirt sound alive, and the ground moved and swelled with the insects. "Well, we're close enough for an easy burial. You can throw the bike over the fence, and it'll land right on the family plot."

"Be quiet." He pulled a greasy rag out of his back pocket and unscrewed something.

"When'd you get back?" Cissy asked.

"Couple of weeks ago."

"How come?"

"I don't know. I guess I missed it here. Ought to lock me up, but it's the truth."

"What about Lucille?"

Jonas frowned. "She and Ray are getting hitched next month, you know. I . . . uh . . . I'm used to it, now." He raised an eyebrow and shrugged. "Ma's fixing a nice supper for your homecoming."

Cissy shivered. She didn't know if she could face Ma.

"What was Denver like?" Jonas asked.

The sob welled up and spilled out before Cissy could stop it. She covered her face with her hands, wanting to stop the tears, but they flowed down her cheeks and around her fingers.

"Don't cry, little sis. It's all right," Jonas whispered in her ear. "I won't let her hurt you anymore. I promise. I know I been bad about that in the past. And I'm more sorry for it than you can ever know."

"No, Jonas. *I* won't let her hurt me anymore. I won't let anyone hurt me anymore."

"Good for you." Jonas looked out over the dried fields, then turned back to the motorbike. He revved the engine until it stopped its guttural snorts and slid into an even growl. "We'd best get back."

As they came into the yard, Fairbanks bounded out of the vegetable garden, his nose covered in dirt.

"He likes digging up the turnips," Jonas said.

The screen door slammed like a gunshot. Cissy felt her mother, felt how she smoldered in her silence. She looked up and caught Ma's stare behind the screen door, caught Daddy looking everyplace but at his family.

Daddy stopped in front of Cissy and shoved a wad of dollar bills in her hand. "Go on inside. Your ma's waiting for a hug."

Jonas slowly stood up from the bike, brushing his hands on his pants and then swinging them at his sides with a barely contained threat. "She'll go in when she's good and ready."

Frank pulled his shoulders back and spread his legs. "Big man of the family now, are you?" He looked Jonas up and down, and a shadow of something terribly sad crossed his face before he hid behind his lying salesman's smile. "You take care of Cissy and your ma, you hear?"

"Sure," Jonas said. "We all know you ain't gonna do it. Now why don't you leave while I'm still in a good mood. And you know what? None of us want you back."

Frank's smile faded. He swallowed, looked around him, then quietly returned to the car.

It was as if nothing had happened. No running away, no city lights and torch singers with funny smiles, no Chinese food or trolley cars, no contest. No Vera.

Cissy stared at the fried potatoes and roasted pork on her plate. Cissy wondered where Ma got the money for the meat. And she knew, quick as she wondered, that Daddy had given Ma enough money to take her back.

The bare bulb above the table swung slightly as a draft slid under the kitchen window. Cissy watched its light and shadow pass over the edges of her food. Ma sat at the head of the kitchen table, only a glass of water in front of her.

Jonas stabbed the meat on his fork. "It's good, Ma. Good roast."

"It's special for Cissy's birthday," Ma said. "She doesn't like it, though."

Cissy felt the pull of Ma's quicksand. "I'm just not hungry."

"Big city girl, now? Used to caviar and champagne?"

"Come on, Ma," Jonas said. "She ain't hungry."

"Well, don't beg to me when you are."

"I never begged you for anything and I won't start now," Cissy said quietly.

"Tarns got some poison trucked in," Jonas cut in. "We're going to start laying it tomorrow morning. It's got banana oil in it. Some fool thinks grasshoppers like banana oil."

Cissy slid her chair back and stood up. A leg caught on an uneven board, and the chair tumbled backward. Cissy froze, waiting for Ma's hand on her. When she didn't feel it, she set the chair upright. "I'd like to go lay down awhile."

"Wait a minute." Ma held out her hand. "Give me the money he gave you."

"Why? It's mine."

"What do you need it for?"

"Ma, come on," Jonas said. "It's her birthday present."

Ma thought about this for a moment, then

reached behind her and slid open a drawer. "This letter came for you some time back."

"For me?" Cissy snatched it from Ma's grasp. "It's from Beth!" She looked at the date. "I was here when this letter came. Why didn't you give me the letter? You knew how much I was waiting for a letter from Beth."

"It slipped my mind."

Of course. Ma and her slippery mind.

Cissy took the letter to read upstairs in private. Fairbanks followed at her heel. Her bedroom shocked her. She expected her old room, filled with movie star pictures and newspaper clippings, but the walls stood bare and white. Cold and frozen like Ma. Ma had wiped her out of existence. She sat on the bed, not knowing what to do, or who she was. She walked to the dresser, then turned away from the mirror that reflected a face she didn't know.

Vera's scarf still lay on the bedstand, the white crane wrapped around the furniture's edges, the mountain hidden in a fold. Cissy picked up the lamp, ripped the scarf off the little table, and stuffed it in a dresser drawer. She then ripped Vera's letter from her dress and threw it in the drawer, too.

"You promised me everything would be all right, Vera. You *promised*."

❧ ❧ ❧

Dearest, Best Beth,

I couldn't have wanted a better birthday present than your letter. And I finally have your address to send all these letters I've written you! Your daddy's hauling cargo at the Long Beach shipyard? Sounds like very hard and exciting work. I wish I could see the ocean, too. You're very lucky, Beth.

Adventure over, Beth. I'm back in Ransom. It sure is nice to have the quiet. You can't believe how noisy Denver was, and how much I missed—

No, Beth, I'm not going to lie. I'm going to tell you the truth, because you're my best friend. Aunt Vera didn't want me anymore. She gave me a letter, but I'm not ready to read it. I never want to hear anything from her again. I hate being a kid—if I was grown-up, I could just hop on Jonas's motorcycle and go someplace else. Be some-one else.

I'm so scared to be here; everything is just the same as when I left—except my room that Ma whitewashed just to punish me, I'm sure. I never told you this before, but Ma used to punish me a lot. Remember how I'd tell you I fell down, or bumped my head on the cupboard? That wasn't what hap-pened. Maybe you guessed it, because you saw Ma angry sometimes.

But I'm not going to let her do it any-more. I'm fourteen now. I'm not a baby, and I can take care of myself.

I so wish you were here, because it's been terrible without you. I haven't had any other friends since you. Why'd you all have to pick up and move?

I don't want to see anyone here, not even Rusty. Funny, I practically forgot about him. I just want to crawl under the bed and stay in the dark. Thank God that Jonas is back home. I don't know what I'd do without him.

I may not send this letter. I wouldn't want to worry you.

Yours always,
Cissy

Chapter Thirty

The morning sun stretched wide and flushed across the flat land, curling purple shadows around the men out in the Tarnses' field. Jonas's figure stood out, bigger, and stronger than when he left home. He stood on a cart, holding on to the barrel of poison, as Ray Tarns and his sons, Ray Jr. and Rusty, pulled the heavy gear across the ground.

Cissy crossed her arms on the windowsill and sighed. Jonas must have swallowed a lot of pride to be out in that field, working for Ray Tarns. He did it for her and Ma, so they could eat. Her brother had grown up.

Farther off, the cottonwoods clung to the banks of the dried creek, not giving up, waiting patiently for the river to provide sustenance again. This land was so deep in Cissy's bones, she felt that she could lie down and be mistaken for the earth. Or be buried by it.

She daydreamed of tall, golden wheat, as it had once been and would be again, caressed by the breezes. She saw people coming back to their homes to take up a hoe or a thresher, right where they'd left the machines when the wind parched the dirt.

But she couldn't see herself. It was like she didn't exist, like she didn't belong here. Where did she belong?

It had been a week since she'd been dropped back into Ransom. Every day, she waited for Ma to hit her. There had been so many reasons—and no reason—Ma had lashed out at her in the past. Luckily, nothing bad had happened. Instead, Ma sent her to town to buy soap and sugar and meat. Ma seemed to be satisfied with the money Daddy had given her. And satisfied that she had an errand and chore girl to do her bidding. It seemed, even, that Ma was trying to behave herself. And yet each hour's peace was fragile; Cissy could never trust Ma.

"Not dressed yet?"

Cissy jumped at the sound of Ma's voice. "Didn't hear you come in."

Ma already looked like she had been up for hours, weary from the day, gray around the eyes and mouth. "I'll need you to go down in the cellar and bring up some jars of peaches."

"Yes, ma'am."

"So, I suppose Vera's forgotten all about you. Not even a call. I'm not surprised. She always was selfish."

Ma's comments seemed offhand, yet they were sharp as a knife. They were meant to cut, and they did.

"No, she's not."

"Not what? Forgotten all about you, or not selfish?"

Cissy clamped her mouth shut. Her thoughts of Vera had become jumbled and confused during the past week. She hated her one minute, missed her the next, dreamed of her each night.

Ma reached into the pocket of her apron. "I have something for you. For your birthday. I know it's a bit late." She started to hand Cissy a small box, wrapped in brown paper, then hesitated and set it on the bedstand.

Cissy stared at it, not sure what to do.

"I was going to send it to Denver," Ma said. "Open it. Be careful with the wrap—I can use it again."

A single strand of pearl and garnet beads lay coiled inside. Grandma's necklace, passed on to Ma. Cissy remembered Ma wearing it on the days Daddy came home from his business trips, those special rare days when Ma dressed in her Sunday best, made fried chicken or pot roast, and allowed

Jonas and Cissy to lick the chocolate-cake batter right out of the mixing bowl.

"You used to wear this for Daddy."

"He won't be coming home anymore," Ma said. "You might as well take it."

"I don't want it."

"Sell it, then."

"You would have given this to Violet, if she were alive, wouldn't you? How much money did Daddy give you to take me back?"

"Enough."

Cissy set the necklace back in the box and slid it across the bedstand. "I don't want it." She needed nothing from Ma anymore.

That night, Cissy sat on the bed in her empty room, Vera's letter lying in her lap. She felt a rush of nausea just looking at it. Her hands were clammy and shaking, so she steadied her breath, then opened the envelope. Aunt Vera's big writing spilled all over the pages. The ink spread into blue lakes of sadness where Vera's tears had dried on the page.

Dear Cissy,

It's late. You're sleeping and wool-gathering, with a little smile on your face. It won't be there tomorrow, that I know. But I want you to understand why I let Frank take you back.

I know you might not forgive me. I know you'll probably hate me. But honey, as hard as this may seem, it is for the best.

We didn't have any money, Cissy. Even before I lost the job at the diner, we were out of money. And that letter came from the school, and it asked for so much, more than I could ever afford. How was I possibly going to give you all I wanted to give you? I saw Frank—he told me that I was in no place to raise a child. He promised me you'd be taken care of, that he'd make sure Rose wouldn't hurt you anymore. Cissy, I tried so hard to make things right. But there was no money. How could I take care of two of us when I didn't even have enough for one? You don't deserve poverty.

Honey, I want to tell you the truth about something. There's been too many lies in our family. You're entitled to some truth. About Maxine and me. We love each other. It wasn't what either of us wanted, it just happened, and honey, I have been so afraid to tell you about it. So afraid you'd hate me.

Frank says living the way I do corrupts you. I don't want to corrupt you. He says that Maxine and I are sick. Is loving someone ever sick?

I have failed you. I wanted to give you the world. I love you, Cissy. I hope, someday, you will forgive me, or at least understand.

You are my heart—

Vera

The thudding in Cissy's head took on the sound of a giant swarm of insects. She crumbled the letter and threw it on the floor. Vera lost her job. So what? She could have found another one. How could she think that sending Cissy back here was best for her? And why did Daddy give Ma money to keep her, and not just give it to Vera? Vera didn't try to fight for her. No—she didn't want Cissy. That was it, plain and simple. Cissy was just another mouth to feed. Vera didn't want to give Cissy "the world." That was just a pretty lie.

What Vera wanted was to be left alone with Maxine. Stupid Maxine. She was all Vera wanted, really.

Because if Vera wanted Cissy, she would have fought for her. She would have given up Maxine and found another job and not sent Cissy back to this miserable little town. She would not have sent Cissy back to Ma.

If Vera really loved Cissy, she would have at least called. Ma was right. Vera had forgotten her.

Chapter Thirty-one

"Hand me the wrench."

"It's too hot, Jonas. Let's go into town and get a NEHI." Cissy swatted a fly from her nose. She leaned against the barn wall—or what was left of it—fanning herself with a movie magazine Mack had dropped by earlier. "I hope they find a teacher for the school soon. I'm getting bored out here."

"Only thing can bore you is yourself."

"Funny, Jonas."

Out in the yard, Fairbanks let out a long howl. Cissy looked through a wide space between two slats. What she saw stopped her heart. "Oh, my God. It's Aunt Vera."

"What?" Jonas joined her.

"I got to get out of here. I don't want to see her."

Aunt Vera stood at the front gate. She seemed afraid to come in. Her eyes flitted around the yard,

201

and when they rested on the barn, Cissy leaned into a shadow. Then Vera straightened her shoulders, took a deep breath, swung the gate open, and marched up to the house.

Ma opened the screen door, then shut it behind her, blocking Vera's way. "What are you doing here?"

"I've come for my daughter."

"Your daughter? That's a laugh. Go back to Denver, Vera."

"No, Rose, I want my daughter. *Mine*. I gave in to you and Frank thirteen years ago—I'm not going to do it again."

"You think you can waltz out here and drag her away?" Ma asked. "She's staying here, Vera. Away from your filth."

Vera stepped back off the porch. Her eyes searched the yard. "Where is she?"

She took a step toward the barn.

"Jonas," Cissy whispered, "I got to get out of here. I can't—I don't understand."

Jonas remained glued to a crack, staring out at Vera. "Shh."

Ma followed Vera into the yard. "Get out. You've never been anything but trouble, Vera. Ever. Get out."

Vera whirled on Ma. "You want her for the money. I want her because I love her. I'm her mother. And I'm tired of lying to please you and Frank."

"I'm the one who fed her and clothed her and gave her a home. You have no right, Vera, no right."

"*You* have no right," Vera said. "You had no right to take her in the first place. You had no right to beat her because she lived and Violet died. So you tell me where she is, Rose."

Run. The word burned in Cissy's head. She darted out of the barn, past Vera, past the open gate, onto the gravel, out to the road. Her lungs filled with hot air and dust; her heart pounded in her throat. She ran across the fields under the sky that didn't end. Toward where? Toward what? She ran so fast, Jonas couldn't catch her. She ran into town, raced past the Hasty Twins butcher shop. Her breath grew ragged, her legs felt light as feathers, but losing strength. Mack, standing on his ladder, changing the movie sign, was only a blur. In the cool blue-black shade of the old Coronado Hotel, her legs gave out. She bent down, hands on her knees, pulling in gulps of air.

Jonas rolled up beside her. He wiped his forehead with his sleeve, then put his hand on her back, comforting her as she regained her strength.

She pulled in a deep breath. "She's my mother?"

Jonas looked down at his feet, then at Cissy. "Yeah."

"And you never told me?"

"It wasn't my place," he said. "I mean, you came and you were my sister. That's it. It didn't make any difference that you had a different mother and father."

"A coward."

Jonas said nothing. They sat side by side in the empty shadows of the hotel, staring across the street at Mason's Emporium and Grocery. The sounds of a radio eased out the open door, and Cissy remembered how Lucille Mason used to flirt with Jonas. It seemed such a long time ago, a lifetime, when she was a different person.

Vera was her mother. The thing she had longed for, wished for, was actually true. But Vera had given Cissy away. Not once, but twice.

Cissy dropped her head in her hands and closed her eyes. She wanted to shut out the world, with its lies and hurts and cruelty. She imagined herself as someone else, some other girl who lived far away from Colorado. She saw herself in yellow sunshine, throwing a ball, near a great, blue, rolling ocean. She wore a new dress with red ruffles. And she had so much money, no one needed to give her away.

She imagined a new mother, a mother like Marmee in *Little Women*. Someone with laughing, crinkly eyes and a soft smile. Someone who hugged Cissy for no reason except that she was there. Like Vera did.

Cissy opened her eyes. She saw Mack talking to Vera. Vera's pink dress snapped in the wind like a silly flag; she looked out of place and slightly ridiculous.

"I'll go tell her to leave you alone," Jonas said.

"No."

"Want me to stay?"

"It's all right, Jonas. I'll be all right."

Jonas got up and brushed off his pants. "If you need anything—"

"No. I need to do this myself."

"Okay."

"Jonas?"

"Yeah?"

"You're the best brother anyone could have."

Cissy waited on the cool steps as Vera approached. Vera limped a bit from walking in heels too high for Ransom. Their eyes met. A surge of energy moved between them. They were part of each other. As much as Cissy didn't want to feel the connection, it was there. It was true and solid.

Vera smiled with her mouth, but not with her eyes. She sat down next to Cissy and looked out at the street. "You'd think they'd plant trees here for some shade, wouldn't you?"

"Yeah."

Vera took in a breath. "When I was fifteen, I gave away the best thing that ever happened to me. Because I was scared and young. And every night, for thirteen years, I cried over my mistake. I wanted to take back all those years. I wanted to feel you as a baby in my arms and then watch you grow up. Not visiting you every month, but watching you change hour by hour. I wanted to take back all the lies. And I tried. And then I gave you up again. Because I was scared." Vera looked at Cissy. "I'm tired of being scared. I'm tired of the lies and excuses and secrets. I'm your mother. I love you more than my own life. And I want you with me. I know I don't have any money, but I'll find another job. And I know that you don't trust me, but I'll prove you can. So here it is: Maxine and I are going to live together, and we want you to live with us. I love Maxine and I love you. That's the person I am. I'm not going to be ashamed of it anymore."

"Where are you moving?" Cissy asked.

"Los Angeles. By the ocean. If that's all right by you."

"Is that near Long Beach?"

"Very close."

"How could you leave me with Ma? You know what she did, and you left me there."

"I'm sorry."

"You're sorry? You're *sorry*?"

"I didn't feel I had a choice at the time. But

now there is." Vera took Cissy's hand in hers. She turned it over, touching each finger with her own. "Look at our hands. So exactly alike."

"What if you leave me again?"

"I won't."

"I don't trust you," Cissy said.

"I know." Vera let go of Cissy's hand. "Does it bother you about Maxine and me?"

Cissy thought about it. She thought it should bother her, but somehow it didn't. It was just love. It made Vera happy. She shook her head.

"Listen. I'm going to go down to the Blue Willow and get you a grape NEHI. And I'm going to sit there, honey, until you decide what you want to do. Whatever you choose, I'll live with." Vera stood. She touched Cissy's cheek. "I love you." Then she walked away. Not looking back.

Cissy waited for Vera to go into the Blue Willow, then she walked down the street toward the Odeon. She found Mack inside the projection room, loading the reels for a new movie.

"I have an idea for the Odeon," she said. "I went to a lot of picture shows in Denver, and the theaters all have velvet curtains that slide back right before the lights go down. Sort of stretches out the anticipation, so you can hang on to that feeling a little longer."

"Velvet curtains? It'd break my budget."

"Seems everybody knows about Vera being my mother but me. I'm a big fool, aren't I?"

Mack dusted the spokes of the projector with a small brush, then loaded a reel. Cissy sat on the stool.

"What's the film?"

"*Naughty Marietta.*"

"I've seen it," she said. "It's good. You'll draw a crowd."

Mack set to work on the second projector. "I would have married Vera, you know. I was sweet on her. But she wanted out of Ransom, and out she went. Off to Denver. She was always looking for something else. And when she came back here—in trouble—well, I still would have married her. She wouldn't have me."

"How come she left me?"

"Frank convinced her that the best thing she could do was to let you grow up in a regular household. He's a heck of a salesman. He could charm money off a corpse. And God forbid anyone in Ransom should find out that a Funk committed a sin. Vera didn't have any money, she didn't have anything. So she gave you up. She was a kid herself." He finished loading the reel and turned to Cissy. He put his hand on her shoulder and said, "Are you a big fool for not knowing about Vera or a big fool for wanting to stay here? She loves you. She was afraid."

"She's a coward."

"Maybe. But one thing I know is she loves you. She gave you up out of love—and it nearly tore her heart to pieces. We all make choices in life, some right and some not. We try to do the best we can with what seems right at the time. And sometimes we're haunted by the path we didn't take. And we have regrets about what we left behind. Be careful what you choose to leave behind. Now, why don't you sit out front, and I'll give you your own VIP screening of the movie."

Cissy sat down with Mack and watched Jeannette McDonald and Nelson Eddy sing silly love songs to each other in even sillier costumes. She thought about Vera, her eyes so dark, her pink dress too bright, a mother missing half her heart. Because she was Vera's other half. She remembered how hard Vera tried to make things better for her, how she took care of her, sewing her dresses, talking about boys with her. How she made Cissy a part of the world and showed her she was a worthwhile person. And she remembered it was Vera who showed Cissy her own strength.

When the second reel finished rolling, she turned to Mack. "You know what? I'm awful thirsty for a grape NEHI."

"Okay, then. I'll see you around, right?"

"Sure, Mack."

"You know, families are made of screwy pieces that don't look like very much to anyone else. But as long as you've got love, you're ahead of the game."

Cissy hugged Mack a long, long time. Finally, he pulled away and said, "You're something else, Cissy Funk. Now, go on before she drinks that cafe out of coffee."

As she walked out of the theater, her body felt as limitless as the horizon. And she knew that at the end of the road, at the door to the Blue Willow cafe, Vera would reach out her hand and help Cissy step off her island. Vera. Her mother.

Dear Beth,

I hope you're doing all right at your new school. Every time I walk down the hall at my school, I pretend you're right around the corner, ready to jump out and scare me. Everything's new and big here—I have my own locker and about twenty different teachers. I met another new girl. Her name is Mary and she lives down the street from me. She's very nice (of course, not as nice as you are), and we have homeroom and algebra together.

When you visit next week, Beth, you'll get to see our new house. And we'll have fun— you and me, and Vera and Maxine and

Fairbanks. The house is a dinky thing, but I have my very own bedroom with a palm tree smack outside the window. I'm happy.

I love you, Beth. And that's the most important thing there is!

Yours always,
Cissy Funk